SCATTERED MOMENTS IN TIME

A Collection of Short Stories & More

SAMANTHA COLE

NOTE FROM AUTHOR

When I began my exciting journey into the world of indie publishing, I had no idea where it would take me. Now, three and a half years later, I can honestly say I've grown tremendously as an author, and I look forward to many more years of sharing the stories and characters who reside in my mind. Since my first published book, I've taken part in several writing contests and anthologies, some of which were never published for one reason or another. I decided to gather them all into one collection and *Scattered Moments in Time* was created. The followers of my books and series will find I've expanded my writing and gone out of my comfort zone for several of the essays and short stories. Such as life, not everything has a happy ending. I hope you can accept how some of these were written, as the characters took me in directions out of my norm. They come from the heart and may have you feeling emotions you didn't expect. I hope you enjoy reading them as much as I enjoyed writing them.

*** *Stoke the Flames* was previously released in the multi-author anthology, Down & Dirty, which is no longer in publication. All rights have been returned to the author.

PART ONE

UNCONDITIONAL: LOVE LIKE A DOG

*H*umans. They sure are funny creatures. Instead of just using their mouths to eat their food from their plates, they use silver things. They do their business in those white, oversized, water bowls, instead of drinking from them. While my kind has fur, they cover themselves with what they call clothes. When they meet, they shake hands instead of sniffing each other. I mean, really, how are they supposed to know if someone is a friend or foe without sniffing them?

My name is Jinx. While many of the dogs in my neighborhood are pure-breeds, my human tells everyone I'm a *Heinz-57* dog. I didn't know what that meant at first, but, apparently, it's because my mom, dad, and grandparents were not worried about each other's pedigree. They didn't think one breed was better than another and chose their mates without bias. My vet—I shudder just thinking of him because he likes to give me shots in my rear end—believes I am part Labrador Retriever, part Staffordshire Terrier, and part something-he-can't-quite-figure-out. But my human thinks I'm a one-hundred-percent mush-ball. I've never met another mush-ball, so I don't know if I look like one. Maybe someday I'll get to see a picture of one or meet a mush-ball at the dog park. I hope I'm not the only one.

Hang on a second. I need to stretch a bit. *Ahhh*, downward dog . . . aaaaand . . . upward dog. Much better. I've noticed you humans have copied our stretches for yourselves. Good thinking. It gets the blood circulating and the kinks out. Okay, now rotate. Once. Twice. And lay back down in the sunbeam shining through the living room window. Perfect.

All right, where was I? Oh, that's right, the dog park. It's a great place to go socialize and catch up on some gossip and chase a few tennis balls. So many dogs to sniff with so little time. My human, Debbie, takes me there a few times during the week, and we always have a lot of fun. She plays fetch with me for a bit before going to talk with her own kind, while I strut my stuff for the lady dogs, hoping to hook up with one. I haven't gotten lucky yet, but I'll keep trying. There's this poodle named Fifi I've got my eye on, but she seems more interested in a bulldog named Butch. A nice guy, that Butch, but I honestly don't know what Fifi sees in him.

What's that? You want to learn more about Debbie? Why, she's the greatest human in the world! She rescued me from jail and gave me a good home. What? Yes, yes, I was in jail, but it wasn't my fault. At least, I don't think it was. I was very little back then, so my memory is a bit fuzzy. What I do remember is when my siblings and I were a few weeks old, and no longer relying on our mom for food, humans came to our home to adopt us. Mom said it was okay because we were old enough to find our forever homes and the humans would become our new families. That's the way things were done.

But the human who adopted me wasn't very nice. I tried to do everything right, but if I had an accident or did something I didn't know I wasn't allowed to do, I got yelled at. I was also home a lot by myself, and it was so lonely. I know Mom said it would be okay, but it didn't feel okay. One day, my human took me on a car ride and brought me to the jail. He told the people there that he didn't want me anymore. They didn't understand why, but they took me in anyway. I was so scared, but the humans in jail were very nice to me. They petted me, took me for walks, and feed me well. But every night they went home and the other dogs and I were left in our rooms. It was dark and frightening. Some of the other dogs cried while a few were angry and growled. I prayed I wouldn't have to stay there long.

Wait! Did you hear that? No, never mind. For a moment there I thought I heard the ice cream man. I *love* the ice cream man. All the kids in the neighborhood get a treat from him, and I get anything that falls to the ground. That is if I'm fast enough.

Anyway, back to what I was talking about. I think I was in jail a little over a week, although it felt longer in dog years, before Debbie walked through the door one day. All week, whenever humans came to look us over, I tried to look playful, friendly, and happy, hoping one of them would adopt me like a few of the other dogs, but that day I wasn't feeling very playful or friendly or happy. Actually, I was very depressed. I didn't want to be there anymore, but I didn't know when I'd be allowed to leave. When Debbie stopped in front of my room, she tilted her head as she stared at me. I didn't have much hope she would want me, so I stayed curled up in a ball in the far corner. But then to my surprise she didn't move on . . . oh, no, not at all. She . . . oh, my goodness, she squatted down and said hello to me. Me! She wanted to meet me!

My tail started wagging all on its own. I picked my head up, hoping beyond hope that this wasn't a dream. And then, oh my, she called me over. Slowly, I stood and took a few shy steps toward her.

"Hey, little guy," she said softly. "Come here. I won't hurt you. You're a handsome boy."

Handsome? Everyone else had called me cute, but she called me handsome! I was in love with her for that word alone. When I reached the barrier keeping us apart, she reached through the bars and scratched my ears. It felt wonderful! I sniffed her hand before licking it. She was a good human, I knew it in my heart.

One of the jailers came over to us. "That's Jinx. He's such a sweet boy, but his owner didn't have time for him. He's neutered and up-to-date on all his shots, but he needs some house-training."

My head dropped in embarrassment, because I knew that meant I had accidents in the house. I really tried to hold it, but sometimes poop happens.

"I think he's perfect. Can I fill out the adoption papers now?"

Oh, well . . . wait, what? Adoption papers? That meant she wanted me. Oh, joy! I barked at her, "Thank you, thank you! You won't regret it! I'll be the best friend I can be!"

And that's how Debbie Shaw became my human eight months ago. I'm so lucky she rescued me, and she tells me every day how glad she is that she found me. But sometimes I get the impression I'm not enough for her. Don't get me wrong, I couldn't ask for a better human, but why settle for one when you can have two, right? At the park, I meet so many dogs who have two or more humans at home who love them and each other. I want that for Debbie and me. I've been keeping my eye out for the perfect mate for her, and I think I finally found him.

His name is Jackson Phelps, and he's our new neighbor. While he doesn't live with any dogs—or cats, perish the thought—he really likes animals, especially me. Debbie and I met him on a walk around the neighborhood last week. He was retrieving his mail from the box at the end of his drive, and, as we approached, he smiled and introduced himself. Before he pet me, he held out his hand so I could get a couple of sniffs in. That's the sign of a good human. We dogs can get very antsy if people try to bypass the sniff test. Anyway, his scent was top-notch, so I let him pet me. Oh, heck, who am I kidding. I liked him so much, I rolled over for a belly rub. Jackson gives awesome belly rubs, but that's not the reason I think he's a good mate for Debbie—although it's a plus. I think they're good for each other because their scents complement each other. It's like kibbles and bits or peanut butter and bacon.

Don't give me that look. Peanut butter and bacon is just as good, if not better than filet mignon, which I've only had once, but it was so yummy. But don't knock my favorite treat until you try it. Next time you cook bacon, dip it in some peanut butter. You'll love it—trust me on this. Anyway, as I was saying, Debbie and Jackson are perfect for each other.

Whoops! It's time! I hear the mailman. I know other dogs bark and growl at the mailman, but I like him. He brings me a biscuit every Friday. I wish he would bring one every day, but Debbie says I'd get fat if that happened. Gotta stay looking good for the ladies at the dog park. *Woof.*

Sorry, got off track. Anyway, when I hear the mailman coming, I know it's time to take Debbie for a walk, because that's when Jackson will be coming out of his house to get his own mail. See where I'm going with this? Uh-huh, I thought you would.

Come on, let's go get Debbie. She's in her home office where she works all day. I'm lucky she works from home because that means I can hang out with her. She tells people she's an author, which means she makes up stories. At least that's what I think it means.

I nudge her thigh with my nose. *"Woof."*

Glancing down, she says, "Hey, handsome." That's me, in case you were wondering. "Is it time for our walk already?"

What would she do without me telling her what time it was? *"Woof."*

"All right. Let me just save today's work on the computer, and we are out of here."

Yes! We'll be right on schedule. Yesterday she was working hard and kept telling me to wait a minute. I tried so hard to hurry her along, but by the time we headed out the door, it was too late. Jackson had been going for a car ride and was already pulling out of his driveway.

Funny thing about humans going for car rides. They don't drive with the windows down often unless there's a dog in the car with them. Don't they know how good it feels to have the wind in your hair as you inhale all those great smells?

I stand perfectly still, except for my bouncing butt, while Debbie attaches a leash to my collar. I'm not a fan of either, although they are in my favorite color blue, but Debbie says it's the law, so I obey it. Don't want to end up back in jail or get my human in trouble with the fuzz.

"*Grr. Grrrufff.*" Oops, sorry about that. When we stepped outside, I saw Mrs. Peabody's cat, Clarence, taking the shortcut across our yard again. I wouldn't mind if he wasn't so stuck up, thinking he was better than me.

Ah, perfect! There's Jackson coming out his front door. Okay, I have to get the timing just right. A few sniffs here. A leg lift there. And . . .

"Hi, Jackson. It seems like we're on the same clock every day, meeting out here."

"It's beginning to be the highlight of my day." Squatting down to greet me, he smiles up at Debbie. Yup, I really think he likes her. *Oh yeah, right there.* Gosh, I love when he scratches that spot right above my tail. It's one of the few places I can't reach on my own. "How's the writing going?"

"Great. I should be finishing up the final chapter today and then I'll read through it again, before sending it to my editor. How about you? Busy today?"

Jackson's a cartoonist. He must be a really good one, too, because I heard Debbie tell her friends that his comic strip is in hundreds of newspapers every day. Too bad I can't read. "Well, we have something in common now. My agent has set up a book deal for me. So for the next few months, I'll be doing two or three strips a day until we have enough to publish."

"Oh my gosh, that's great! I love reading your strip every day, so I expect you to sign my copy when I buy it."

Jackson stands. "I think I can spring for a free copy for my favorite neighbor. And I'll definitely sign it for you. On one condition."

Here it comes. Come on, Jackson, ask her if she'll be your mate.

"What condition?" Debbie sounds wary, but she's still smiling.

"If you'll have dinner with me?"

Wait? What? Dinner? That's it? Come on, Jackson. I thought . . . oh well, it's a start, I guess. And, all right! Debbie said yes!

"Great. If you don't mind eating at my place, I'm a pretty good cook. And you can bring Jinx along. No point in him staying home alone."

Told you he was a good guy. *"Woof."*

Debbie laughs. "I think it's okay with him. What time should I come over and what can I bring?"

Peanut butter and bacon?

"Um, how about something for dessert? Say around six?"

Darn it. Dessert means sweet stuff, and Debbie doesn't let me have sweet stuff, which is why I have to be quick when the kids drop their ice cream.

"Sounds perfect. We'll see you then. Come on, Jinx. Let's go get your business taken care of."

A few eons later, Debbie and I are at Jackson's front door, with the brownies she'd baked after our walk. They smell good, but Debbie smells even better. She groomed herself up and sprayed on her special "going-out" scent. It's pretty, just like her, and I hope Jackson appreciates it.

After she rings the doorbell, he opens the door. "Hey, right on time. Wow, you look fantastic. You should wear dresses more often."

Debbie blushes. "Thanks. That's the downside of working at home. You tend to get lazy and spend the day in lounge wear. So whenever I get a chance to get dressed up, I like putting on a skirt or dress. You look nice, too."

And he does. Jackson obviously did some grooming of his own. He smells good too—kind of like . . . *steak?*

"I know what you mean." He clears his throat. I think he's a little nervous, but I'm not sure why. It's just me and Debbie, and we're not a threat. "Not me looking nice. I meant, being lazy. I know what that's like. Here, let me take that from you. Come on into the kitchen. Would you like a glass of wine? Or I have beer, soda or iced tea?"

"Wine sounds great."

Pushing past Jackson, I start sniffing around the place. You can tell a lot about a human by how his home smells and . . . *oh, my, goodness. Is that? Could it be? Filet mignon? It is! Yes! Yes! Yes! Oh, happy day! Okay, Jinx. Calm down, dude. Time to be on your best behavior, and when the time is right, give them the sad, puppy-dog look Debbie can't resist. And maybe, just maybe, you'll get a taste of that yummy stuff.*

After sniffing every square inch of the place, I'm convinced more than ever that Jackson is the perfect mate for Debbie. Trotting into the kitchen . . . *oh, heavenly smells* . . . I lay down on the floor at Debbie's feet. They spend the next few hours talking, eating, and laughing. I didn't hear everything they said because I dozed off a few times—and apparently my snoring got loud a time or two from a few comments Jackson made. For a second, I'd been slightly insulted until he admitted he was a snorer too. A man who admits his faults and pokes fun at himself so the dog doesn't feel bad? Gotta love him.

I lift my head as Jackson says he's been the human for several dogs over the years and his most recent one, Cleo, had sadly crossed over to the Rainbow Bridge a few months before he moved into this new house. Debbie and I both give him our sympathy. Debbie's is verbal, but I decide to make mine more subtle and rest my chin on his foot. He reaches down and scratches my head, but doesn't ask me to move. "I've been thinking it's time to go adopt another one. The house is so quiet without one. Maybe you and Jinx could go to the shelter with me tomorrow and see if any of the dogs there are a good fit. What do you say?"

Say yes, Debbie!

"There's a great no-kill shelter nearby. It's where I found Jinx. I'd love to help you find a new dog, but is it a good idea to bring him along?"

"Well, since we'll probably be joining you on your daily walks, I'd like to make sure he approves of the one we pick out."

Smart man.

"Okay," Debbie agrees to my delight. "Oh, look at the time. I really should be going, but first let me help you clean up."

They both stand as I stretch under the table. "No worries. I've got it. All that's left is just the coffee cups and plates. Can I give this to Jinx?"

What? Give Jinx what? Oh, please, let it be steak!

Debbie laughs. "Sure. And after that, he'll be your friend for life."

Squatting down, Jackson calls me over and, of course, I make a bee-line to him. I can see the small, juicy piece of meat in his hand and as much as I want to lunge for it, Debbie taught me good manners. I sit and lift a paw to Jackson, not waiting for him to ask for it. He chuckles, shakes my paw, and holds out the steak for me. Gingerly, I take it from his hand and as the flavors hit my mouth, I can't help swallowing it in one bite. I really should learn how to savor my food, but when it comes to filet mignon, I doubt I'll ever be able to do it.

While I lick my chops, I follow the two of them to the front door. I stare up at them as they stand on the front steps, suddenly shy around each other. A moment of silence passes between them before they seem to slowly gravitate toward each other and . . . yes! Wahoo! They're giving each other kisses! I love giving kisses!

Um . . . Debbie? Jackson?

Hmmm, maybe I'd better give them a moment and check the area for any pesky squirrels. It looks like it's the beginning a long and beautiful love story. And you can thank yours truly for making it happen.

Woof.

PART TWO

A WARRIOR'S HEART

*T*hud-thump.

No. Please, God, this can't be happening.

Thud-thump.

All around him, the silence roared. Men were dead and dying, but he couldn't hear a sound due to the last blast that'd come too close for him to avoid. The attack had come from out of nowhere. Jokes and laughter had been replaced by screams, barked orders, and moans of pain. Arguments over which teams were going to be in the World Series this year had changed to shouts for a medic. A routine patrol had turned into something far worse than sweating in the unbearable heat.

Five months left on his last tour in Afghanistan. Five more months until he could retire into civilian life. Five more months until the birth of his first child.

His wife and he had been trying for four years without success, but for Christmas, she'd sent him a care package. Inside had been the normal food, toiletries, magazines, and books. A few gag gifts had been included, so when he was unwrapping the last one, he hadn't expected to find a pair of baby booties. Confusion had turned to shock. Shock had turned to elation and then at the top of his lungs, he'd bellowed, "I'm going to be a father!"

Thud-thump.

Shouts of congratulations had filled their barracks, in addition to back slapping and whistles. His captain had grabbed his arm, dragging him outside before taking off at a run. Using his rank and the good news, the man had gotten him to the front of the line of soldiers waiting to Skype back home. It had still been another half hour before he'd ended up face to face on the monitor with his wife. She'd been waiting for over two weeks for him to receive the package and open the contents. At her appointment three days earlier, she'd found out they were going to have a boy. The two of them had spent his total allotted time, laughing, crying, and telling the other how their hearts were filled with love and joy.

Thud-thump.

That same heart now was fighting to continue beating—to remain alive. He couldn't feel anything below his waist, but the thumping in his chest, which was slowing down with each contraction, he was all too aware of. Looking to his left through the smoke and chaos, he saw his captain had already expired. With obvious head injuries, he doubted the man ever knew they'd come under attack, with RPGs raining down on them from the enemy. Others had been thrown violently or torn apart, and the uninjured and walking wounded were doing their best to administer care and battle the insurgents at the same time.

He was dying. He knew it and there was nothing anyone would be able to do to change the inevitable. Anderson, the medic, knelt beside him. He still couldn't hear and had no idea what the man was saying even though he saw his lips moving. Maybe it was false hope, that everything would be okay. Maybe it was a layman's last rites. He didn't know, but he did need to communicate somehow.

Thud-thump.

Opening his mouth, he struggled with what he wanted to say, hoping he would be understood. "L-Letter. L-Lock . . . er."

The words must have come out because the man nodded as he continued to try to keep the life blood from pouring from the battered body before him. It was a request the medic had surely heard and followed through on too many times to count. *Please deliver my death letter to my family. My wife. My parents. My . . . unborn son.*

Thoughts of what he'd wanted to do with the boy filled his mind. Fishing. Playing catch. Teaching him his ABCs and then one day, how to drive. He'd wanted to show his son how to treat a woman with the respect she deserved. That was what his wife had told him first attracted her to him. He'd held doors open. Pulled out chairs. Walked her to the front door after every date. It'd been what his dad had taught all four of his sons to do. Hopefully, the old man would be able to see through his grief and teach his grandson the rules of being a gentleman, in place of the father who wouldn't be able to.

Thud-thump.

What day is it? They all seemed to run together out here in the desert. Someone had said it earlier. Through the darkness trying to overtake his mind, the numbers came to him. *Oh, no. Not today, Lord. Any other day but Valentine's Day. Please. No.*

It was the day he and his wife had met so many years ago. He'd gone out with a bunch of his single buddies to a local pub, and there she'd been, visibly upset. Some jackass she'd been dating for less than a month had stood her up on what was supposed to be the most romantic day of the year. After receiving no answer to her texts and phone calls, she'd gotten up from the table for two to leave and promptly spilled her purse. Being the gentleman his father had raised, he'd rushed over to help her. When she'd looked up at him with frazzled, tear-filled, brown eyes, he'd known he was a goner. His heart had been hers from that moment on.

17

Two years later, he'd proposed on the same day. Cliché, yes, but she hadn't been expecting it. He'd enlisted the help of a few buddies and the principal of the school where his wife still taught first grade. Her class was brought to the auditorium where she thought there was going to be a "Military Day" with soldiers from the base. But instead, when the curtain went up, there he stood in his dress uniform. With his friends playing the piano and two acoustic guitars, he'd serenaded her with "Me And You," by Kenny Chesney, before getting down on one knee to propose. After she finally stopped crying, she'd said yes to the delight of her eighteen students as well as her folks, who'd been hiding behind the curtain.

Thud-thump.

They had wanted to have a Valentine's Day wedding too, but the military hadn't accommodated them. So on November 1st, they'd tied the knot in front of their family and friends, three weeks before he'd deployed again. That first tour, after they'd started dating, and the subsequent ones during their marriage, had been hard on both of them, but thanks to their letters, emails, phone calls, and Skype, they had made it through. And each time he arrived home to her loving arms, he thanked God for bestowing upon him the greatest woman he could've ever asked for.

This time was different though. This Valentine's Day his wife would become a widow with a child on the way. He wished he could have seen her one more time. Her eyes. Her smile. The way she crossed her arms and cocked her hip to the side when she was exasperated with him for some reason. He wanted to be there for when she would be screaming and panting in childbirth. He yearned to hold his son just once. Would he have blue eyes like his dad and beautiful, dark hair like his mother? Would he know how much his father loved him and hated the fact they would never meet? Would the boy know the dying man's last thoughts were of him and the wife he was leaving behind?

Thud-thump.

After finding out they had a child on the way, he'd revised his death letter. In it, he'd added some notes to be given to the boy when he was old enough. *Lord, please let him forgive me for not being there for him. Let him understand the reasons I had to leave and not to grow to hate the men who'd taken his father from him.* It was hatred that had brought him here in the first place. Hatred for people who thought, dressed, prayed, and lived differently. He wished by the time his son was old enough, there was peace throughout the world. He hoped there would never be a time the boy would experience the perils of war, although he'd be proud if his footsteps were followed. Just not to this point. Not to the point of dying in the name of freedom.

He'd come from a long line of military men. World War I. World War II. Korea. Vietnam. Desert Storm. Operation Iraqi Freedom, which then became known as Operation New Dawn. And finally, what had led him here—the War in Afghanistan. Fathers, sons, grandsons, uncles, cousins, brothers, and even one sister from his family had fought for their country and each returned to grow old in the states. But that was about to change. He would be the first in many generations dating back to the 1800's who wouldn't be walking off a boat or plane and into loving arms at the end of a tour. Instead, his body would be returned within the confines of a pine box, draped with the American flag he'd duly respected and saluted every day. That flag would be folded with precision and handed to his crying wife as an officer thanked her for her husband's service. Taps would be played. Shots would be fired. Fond memories would be told, and a pint or two would be lifted in his honor.

He knew the love of his life well—she was a true military wife. Despite her grief, she would place the triangular bundle of red, white, and blue in a glass and wooden display box, along with his citations. The same medals he'd proudly worn on his dress uniform, as well as the ones he would never personally receive—the Purple Heart, a combat action medal, and any others the powers that be decided to bestow upon him. She would explain to their son what each one meant and how they had been earned. He'd learn how to salute the American flag, say the Pledge of Allegiance, and know the sacrifices made so others could be free.

Thud-thump.

It was getting harder to breathe. The time he had left was becoming shorter with each desperate beat of his heart. Anderson had done what he could before moving on to the next mortally-wounded man. Another person had taken the medic's place by his side. The new kid. Nowicki, wasn't it? He was on his first tour and was still wet behind the ears as they say. But despite his ashen face, painted with dirt, grime, and blood, the boy had become a man today and clasped his dying brother's hand while praying for his soul. Would this be his son one day? Scared out of his mind, but compassionate enough to fake it?

How many more wars would take place in this world before the human race destroyed itself? Was peace just an illusion? A fantasy someone had created thousands of years ago, just to give people false hope? No. He knew good will existed. He'd seen it many times in his life and had been on the receiving end on numerous occasions.

A few months ago, the night before this last deployment, he'd taken his wife out to their favorite restaurant. Nothing fancy, but that was how they liked it. Relaxed and homey appealed to them more than crystal champagne glasses and fine china. He'd still been in his uniform from an earlier meeting and, because it'd been getting late in the evening, he'd opted not to change. While waiting for their food, they'd chatted and held hands, wishing time would slow down so they'd have a few more hours before saying goodbye. A young boy of nine or ten came over to their table and handed him a note, before saluting and then returning to his seat a few tables away. When his wife and he had looked over at the family consisting of a mother, a father, a set of grandparents, and two children, the older man just nodded and winked in their direction while the others smiled. Opening the note, he and his wife had found words of kindness, prayers for his safe return from wherever he may be going, and gratitude for his service. The kicker had been their meal had been paid for. Neither one of them had been able to keep their tears at bay.

Thud-thump.

That hadn't been an illusion. A fantasy. It'd been real. That family respected the flag and those who sacrificed everything in the name of God and country. In his heart, he knew someday his wife would see a young couple, with one or both of them dressed in a military uniform, and she would send their son over with a note that said, *Thank you for your service. Your meal has been paid for. It's the least we could do for keeping us safe. We'll be praying that God will watch over you and return you to your loved ones.*

Those words resonated through his mind as his sight dimmed. They had not been written in vain. The afterlife was waiting for him. He knew it. The last moments of his life on earth had come. Soon he would be watching over his wife as she gave birth to their son. He'd do his best to guide the boy as he grew, and he'd pray his child would know only peace. But if that wasn't possible, he hoped the proud warrior's heart, which had been passed down through generations, would beat in his son's chest until he was old and grey.

NUMBERS DON'T LIE

*S*igh. Cora Bishop stepped off the offensive scale and watched the needle swing back to zero, a far cry from where it had been moments earlier. Today was her fiftieth birthday, and at two hundred and ten pounds, while standing five-foot-seven, those numbers combined into a depressing mess of vital statistics. She was what her mother had always described as 'big boned', but the bitchy bullies she'd known in high school had just called her fat. *Well, Cora, the numbers don't lie—but now you're old and fat.*

Holding the towel, which she'd donned after her shower, she shuffled out to the bedroom were Frederick, her Siamese cat, lay atop the covers, quietly grooming himself. He had multiple personalities, ranging from a cuddly animal who adored his owner to pretending she didn't exist. Today he was leaning toward the latter. Dropping her towel, she avoided her reflection in the dresser mirror and threw on her underwear, bra, jeans, and a comfortable, black sweater. When her body was completely covered, it was only then that she checked her appearance. Not bad, but far from great. A touch of makeup and styling her long, brown hair would help.

Three hours and half a dozen boring errands later, she began to head home in her eight-year-old Honda, which had seen better days. While she couldn't afford a brand new one, a gently used, former lease would probably be perfect for her. Making the decision to start looking for a new vehicle, she wasn't aware of the police car with its lights on behind her until the siren let out a short bark. *Damn it.* Glancing at her speedometer, she groaned—fifteen miles per hour over the posted speed limit. *Great.* Just what she needed to make the depressing day even worse—a ticket.

Pulling over to the side of the road, she remembered everything her ex-husband had told her to do if she was stopped by the police. She made sure she was far enough on the shoulder so the officer wouldn't have to stand in the roadway, then she rolled the window down, turned off the engine, and rested her hands on the steering wheel. This all helped the officer conclude that she wasn't a threat.

The crunching of feet on the gravel had her turning to see the uniformed man approach her driver's window with a stern expression on his face. Well, what she could see of it, since he had reflective sunglasses on. Pasting on a smile, she hoped he would let her off with a warning. "Hi, officer? Did I do something wrong?"

"You were doing seventeen miles per hour over the speed limit, ma'am. License and registration, please."

"Really?" Maybe if she sounded clueless and remorseful, it would help the situation. Just don't cry she told herself. Her ex had said most cops had received the false crying routine so many times, they ignored tears. She dug into her purse for her wallet. "I'm so sorry. I didn't realize I was going that fast."

"I clocked you with the radar, ma'am. The numbers don't lie. I calibrated the unit myself about an hour ago." The tone of his voice was an indication he'd given that short speech many times before. Handing him her license and vehicle registration, she bit her lip. The stress of the day was starting to hit her as he studied her information. Surprisingly, his tone changed. "Well, now, Miss Bishop. I can't exactly give you a ticket on your birthday, now can I? That wouldn't be in the best interest of the public."

Instead of thanking him, Cora burst into tears. She couldn't help it as she covered her face in embarrassment. Her door opened, and through her fingers, she saw the officer crouch down next to her. His voice softened as he rubbed her shoulder. "Hey, now. What's this? I thought you'd be happy I wasn't giving you a ticket, and I don't think these are happy tears."

She shook her head and dropped her hands in her lap. "I'm s-sorry. I don't know what came over me. I just thought my life would be so different when I hit fifty, and it's not. I'm an old, divorced, overweight woman, who bursts into tears because a police officer is nice enough to say he isn't going to give me a ticket because it's my birthday."

His chuckle went through her, warming her unexpectedly. "Fifty, huh? I didn't even look at the year. First off—you don't look a day over thirty-five. And I'm divorced, too, so that just means we didn't marry the right person the first time around. I turned fifty last May, and trust me, the second half of your life is going to be awesome." Her tear-filled gaze met his friendly one. He was a good-looking man, with dark hair peppered with strands of grey. He'd taken his sunglasses off, and she now saw his eyes were brilliant blue. After a quick glance over his shoulder, he turned back to her. "Tell you what, Ms. Bishop. It's about time I took a coffee break. Would you like to join me at the donut shop across the street? As long as you don't make any cop and donut jokes, that is."

What? Is he serious? No, you idiot. He's not asking you out, he just feels bad that you're crying. But her hands were still shaking, and she wasn't up to driving again at the moment, so what harm could be done by having a cup of coffee with the man? "I promise, no jokes."

"Great." He stood and shut her driver's door. "Follow me then."

They parked in the lot and he held the door to the shop open for her. After ordering coffee and a cupcake for both of them at the counter, he insisted on paying for hers. Taking a seat at a table, she accepted the cup and small plate he handed her before sitting across from her. Mumbling a "thank you," she didn't know what else to say and hoped he would fill in the silence.

"I've been trying to figure out where I know you from and I finally got it. You walk laps around the high-school track a few times a week, don't you?"

Oh, great, he's seen me at my sweaty worst, with my big boobs bouncing with every step, along with the rest of me. No matter how much exercise she got, she could never get below a size fourteen and usually hovered in size sixteen, which is where she currently was. Her doctor insisted that despite her size, she was healthy, with all her blood work and vitals within normal range. Cora just wished her outward appearance was an indication of her inner health. She studied him a little closer and realized she'd seen him before as well. "You're usually jogging around the track, aren't you? I didn't recognize you in uniform."

He shrugged. "A lot of people don't know me out of uniform, and sometimes that's not a bad thing."

His gentle smile tugged at her heart. He was really a nice man. Cora tilted her head "I don't even know your name."

"Sorry, I should have properly introduced myself. I lost my name tag on an arrest yesterday and haven't had time to replace it." He reached across the table. "Jim Zaragoza."

Shaking his proffered hand, her eyes narrowed. "Zaragoza? Are you related to Beth?"

He nodded. "Yup. She's my kid sister. How do you know her?"

"We work together on the pediatric ward. I'm a nurse, too."

After taking a sip of his coffee, he smiled, brightening up his already handsome face. "Gotta love a small world." He pointed at the cupcake she had yet to touch. "I wish I had a candle for you to blow out. Everyone deserves one on their birthday."

Her posture sagged. "Yeah, well, it really isn't something I was looking forward to celebrating."

"How come?" When she didn't answer other than a shrug of her shoulders, he rested his crossed arms on the table. "You mentioned you're divorced. Any children?"

"Two boys and a girl, but they're all out on their own now. I have four grandchildren, too."

His grin grew. "I have three grandkids, and two daughters. Are you close to your kids?"

"Of course." She smiled as she thought of her family. There was never a week where she didn't see them on one day or another.

He nodded. "Okay, so you have a great job, which I can tell you love, just by how you said you were a nurse. You're close to your children and grandchildren. With those beautiful eyes and smile, I bet you have a hell of a personality, which means you have a lot of friends, right?"

She could see where he was going with this, and the fact that he liked her smile and eyes made her sitting up a little straighter. "Yes, I have friends I'm close to."

"So what's wrong with turning fifty? It's only a number."

When he put it that way, what *was* wrong with turning fifty? Her family was throwing her a party tomorrow night, but up until now, she hadn't been looking forward to it. Funny. What had started out as a miserable day, had become something completely different thanks to her heavy foot and an alert, but kind, police officer.

They chatted for a little while until his radio squawked, alerting him to a burglar alarm. Standing, he threw out their garbage before walking her to her car. "It was very nice meeting you, Cora, but I have to run. Promise me you'll obey the speed limit and enjoy your birthday. I think there should be a law about that somewhere."

An amused giggle escaped her. "I will. Thanks."

He winked at her, before turning on his heel.

Blushing, she watched him hurry to his car and drive away with a wave in her direction. Sighing, she thought, now why can't I meet a nice guy like that? She doubted he'd be interested in her. He probably already had a girlfriend—one who was a lot skinnier than Cora. Despite that last thought, she decided to take Jim's advice and turn today into a celebration of all that was good in her life, instead of what she didn't like about it.

At five-thirty that evening, she sat on her couch with Frederick in her lap. She'd spent the rest of the day getting a well-deserved manicure and pedicure, before checking out the local car dealer. To her delight, they had been running a special offer to get rid of last year's models and make room for the new. Using the haggling skills her father had taught her years ago, she'd even gotten a better deal, one which made her sign for her new car on the spot. Now, she was settling in for the news followed by a rom/com movie she'd ordered from Netflix. She was looking forward to her birthday bash tomorrow and planned on going shopping in the morning to find a new dress to wear.

Just as a commercial ended and the news anchors came back on, her doorbell rang. Not expecting anyone, she peered out the peephole and saw nothing but the color red. "Who is it?"

"Jim Zaragoza, Cora. From this afternoon."

What? Unlocking and opening the door, she stared in shock at the man who was now dressed in his civilian clothes and holding a large bouquet of roses. "Hi. What are you doing here?"

Grinning, he handed her the driver's license and registration she'd forgotten to get back from him. "I put these in my shirt pocket when you started crying and forgot about them. Then I decided I'd take a chance and see if the birthday girl still had nothing planned for this evening and wanted to go out to dinner with me. What do you say?"

Stunned, it took her a moment to respond as he waited patiently for her answer. Smiling, she admitted, "I say, I think I'm going to enjoy turning fifty. After all it's just a number, right?"

THE LOST MAN

*S*taring out the window, his gaze focuses on absolutely nothing. Things which used to bring him joy, now barely register. The disease which has taken over his brain has robbed him of his memory, his passions, even the love of his life. Although his wife passed away several years ago, Alzheimer's has taken her from him a second time. Now she is only a fleeting memory which confuses him more and more each time it darts through his mind.

Shuffling over to the recliner in the corner of the solarium, he sits and ignores the watchful eye of the facility's caretakers. There are many others like him on this floor of the nursing home. People with blank stares, experiencing bouts of sadness or elation at times when their disease relents and gives them a moment of clarity—however long or brief it might be.

Seconds turn into minutes, minutes into hours and hours into days. No one can comprehend how lost he feels when nothing looks memorable to him. Imagine waking one morning, in a strange bed, in an unfamiliar room, yet the clothes in the dresser are your size, even if you don't recognize them. The face in the mirror is the same as the man in a few family pictures scattered throughout the small room, although it has aged quite a bit since they were taken. Still, you can't recall when and where the photos were taken or who the other people are. Then someone walks in and says, "Good morning, Mr. Fitzgibbons. How are you today?" You look around, trying to figure out who Mr. Fitzgibbons is, because it's not you. Or is it? You're the only one in the room. This is what he goes through almost every day, not that he remembers any of it. No, the disease has made sure each day is new and terrifying as he struggles to find some small item or recollection with which he can connect to his past.

Music floats over from the radio on the other side of the room. The staff has it tuned to an oldies station—not the music from the 60s, 70s, and 80s, but even earlier. The good old days. When life was simpler and carefree. One song ends and another song begins as the first few notes niggle at the far reaches of his mind. As he closes his eyes, letting the tune flow through him, a vision appears before him. Moments from long ago flash by as if they were happening all over again. A baby blue, Ford Fairlane. A pretty brunette, with gentle, brown eyes sitting next to him at a drive-in movie. They share a bucket of popcorn and a bottle of Coca Cola, more interested in each other than what is playing out on the screen in front of them. The evening ends on the front porch of her home as he kisses her for the first time, and swears it won't be the last.

As their high school football team's star quarterback and head cheerleader, they are elected king and queen of the prom. Life after graduation is new and exciting, but even the distance of separate colleges can't damper their love. He majors in business administration, and she studies to become a teacher. A few months after getting their degrees and then jobs in their respective fields, he proposes.

Fast forward a year—that same pretty woman, dressed in white, is walking through a church on her father's arm. In her hands is a bouquet of flowers, but they pale in comparison to the stunning beauty carrying them. As they stand before God, a priest blesses the young couple's union and proclaims to the crowd gathered that they are now man and wife. Rice is thrown, and the clatter of tin cans follow them as they leave on their honeymoon with the rest of their lives spread before them.

Hard work interspaced with loving times is in their future. Anxious pacing in a hospital waiting room, anticipating the announcement of a healthy boy or girl, is a scene which will be played and then repeated three more times over a six year period. Their home in the suburbs is filled with children, laughing and playing. Summer vacations are spent either at the Jersey shore or camping in the Catskill Mountains. Holidays are always big affairs, with everything from him pretending to be Santa to Easter egg hunts and Thanksgiving feasts which could feed an army. Birthdays, anniversaries, and celebrations of every kind are always done in as big a way as they could afford. All of this, and the occasional argument or two thrown in to spice things up, become the norm of their lives.

Then one morning, he wakes to find she has left him, not by choice, but because her time had come. Almost overwhelmed by his grief and the scent of the flowers filling the funeral home, he stands over her casket, committing her weathered face to memory. Little did he know the treasured image would soon fade into oblivion.

Within a year, he is complaining to his children that someone has been coming into his home and hiding things on him. His keys and wallet are constantly missing, only to be found in odd places such as the freezer or in a jacket he swears he hasn't worn in years. The utility companies begin to harass him, refusing to acknowledge he has paid his bills, just like he'd done for years. How dare they say they never receive the checks he vaguely remembers writing.

One day his children and grandchildren call him throughout the morning and afternoon to wish him a happy birthday. He hadn't had the heart to tell them they had all gotten the date wrong. Hadn't they? When did he start having a hard time remembering their names? They visited often, weekly in fact, but each time it was getting more difficult to put a name to a face.

Slowly, but all too quickly, his mind begins to betray him. He can no longer recall people, events, and things which had always held a huge importance in his life. There are days he feels like a child in kindergarten, who doesn't yet know that two plus two is four, making it impossible to balance a checkbook. One moment, he believes Kennedy is still president, then the next, he can't even recall his own name. Was this what it was like to waste away? To cease to exist within one's own mind?

As the three-minute song ends, the brief recollection of a lifetime of memories dwindles away. He slowly opens his eyes and at first he is unsure of what he is seeing, but as the seconds tick by, his foggy mind gradually clears. The room he'd been sitting in moments before is gone and in its place is nothing but a warm, white light that is almost blinding. It dims slightly and a shadow appears. He tries to focus on the figure advancing toward him, and suddenly he recognizes the pretty brunette with gentle, brown eyes and an affectionate smile. She beckons to him, and without hesitation, he rises and takes several steps until he is standing in front of her. Reaching up, he gently caresses her cheek with the back of his hand while their love, and a lifetime of memories flood his mind and heart. As his mortal body takes its last breath, he realizes he is no longer lost, instead, he is finally going home.

PART THREE

THE HATRED WITHIN

*T*aking a deep breath, Jason Young eyed the battery-operated, analog clock someone had hung on the wall. It was the type that could be found in squad rooms and schools anywhere; it had a white face with black numbers. A red second hand ticked slowly, counting down the first minute of a new day. The silence around him was deafening, broken only by the occasional rustling of clothing and squeaking of leather as someone shifted on their feet and the distant sounds of sirens. A rat ran across the dirty floor in search of food, ignoring the two hundred or so men and women gathered in the abandoned warehouse in the bowels of the city. One minute. One more minute until 12:01 a.m. on Friday, September 16th, 2022. To quote President Franklin D. Roosevelt, "A day which will live in infamy."

This was it. Martial law was taking effect in less than one minute. The City of New York Police Department, the largest local law enforcement agency in the United States, established in 1845, was to be no more, along with the departments in many other cities across the nation. Young and his fellow officers, over

40,000 strong in this city alone, had been ordered by the President of the United States to stand down and disband.

Jason flipped his shield over and over in his hand as the seconds ticked by. If the piece of metal could talk, it would tell not only his stories, but those of his father and grandfather. NYPD #1372 had been worn by all three of them. Upon his graduation from the police academy seven years ago, the two men had stood in front of him as Joseph Young had pinned the badge on his grandson's chest, just as he'd done for his son, Stephen, twenty-one years earlier. The pride on their faces was burned into Jason's memory. Thank God they were both deceased now and would never see what had become of the city and country they'd both proudly served.

The stench of smoke and burning rubber hung heavy in the air. The riots still raged throughout the city, just as they did in Detroit, Washington, D.C., Miami, Atlanta, Los Angeles, Dallas, Chicago, and so on. The loss of life had been staggering and the number of dead on both sides of the Thin Blue Line continued to rise. Three of Jason's squad members had been killed during the nationwide coordinated attacks that had taken the lives of over 300 police officers in seventy cities. One of them had been a rookie at the tender age of twenty-three. Another was killed three days before his first son was born.

Being on this side of the Thin Blue Line, the dead officers' names were not constantly being repeated at the top and bottom of every news hour. Their loss only meant something to the brothers and sisters in blue and their families. For the media, it didn't fuel the flames of hatred, and that's what they needed to make money and stay in power. Contrary to what they led you to believe, it was the media that controlled the government, and the irrational federal response to a civil war brought on by false and biased reporting was the proof. The media giants didn't care that the United States lay in ruins as long as they stayed in power and the money kept flowing in.

Tick. Tick. Tick.

Outside, the usual noises of the bustling city that never sleeps had been replaced with explosions, screams, and gunfire. Armored military vehicles rolled through the streets. The USARNG—United States Army National Guard—had been arriving throughout the past few days, preparing to take control of the city. As soon as martial law went into effect, so too did the curfew, with permission to shoot anyone who disobeyed the order. If the protestors thought only certain groups had targets on their backs before all of this, they were in for a rude awakening. They thought people had been shot for the color of their skin, instead of the crimes they'd been committing? Well, just wait until they realized people could be shot just for daring to step outside their homes after curfew.

Tick. Tick. Tick.

12:01. The room seemed to sigh in relief. What the hell had they'd expected to happen? A ticker tape parade down the Canyon of Heroes on Broadway? The ball dropping in Times Square a few months early? A massive air strike that would blow up the entire city?

"All right, listen up."

As Jason rubbed his shield to a shine on the black tactical pants he now wore instead of his blue uniform, his captain stood in front of the dozens of now former NYPD officers. "If anyone wants to back out, this is your last chance. No one will fault you. Your families come first."

Jason glanced around just as everyone else did. They'd all known the score going into this. Hell, they'd been covertly preparing for it for months, as soon as the rumors about Martial Law had been substantiated. At first, everyone thought it was a joke, but when they found out it wasn't, members of law enforcement across the city began stockpiling weapons, ammo, dark clothing, bulletproof vests, and other equipment. They'd studied the underground tunnels throughout the city, which were part of the subways, sewer lines, and every other system that had workings down below. They'd plotted the areas that were less likely to be covered by the National Guard, which would result in a higher number of crimes against innocent victims. The NYPD computer geeks had created an app for the officers' cell phones and tablets, and transferred as much information on every building and business in the city that they could. No matter how much they'd prepared for this day, it hadn't stopped them from praying it would never come.

No one backed out. Instead, they started passing around empty cardboard boxes. One by one the men and women dropped their NYPD shields into them. As of a minute ago, they were no longer officers—they were vigilantes. They would do whatever was needed to defend the city they'd sworn an oath to protect.

As a box was passed down his row, Jason swallowed hard. Never had he thought he wouldn't one day pin #1372 on his son's chest. Joseph Stephen Young was only six years old and had been named after both his grandfather and great grandfather. But as of now, the Thin Blue Line that had run through the Young family for generations was being severed. When the symbolic, cardboard coffin reached Jason, he took one more look at the no longer respected symbol of authority then silently tossed it in with the others, and passed the box along.

"You all know your call numbers and sectors," Captain Delarosa said. "Do whatever is necessary to make it through your shift and protect the innocent. Set your transmission frequencies to channel seven for regular chatter and assignments. But keep the chatter to a minimum—remember, the government is no longer behind us. Channel six is for emergencies. We'll be monitoring channels one through three which are the National Guard channels, as well as four and five which are the FDNY and EMS channels."

Somewhere in the city, there was a headquarters where their

superiors were running this new, nameless group of protectors. It almost sounded like something out of a superhero comic book. Somewhere down the line it would get a name, probably from the media when they found out about it. It was going to be interesting to see the spin they would eventually put on it.

Every ambulance now had two armed military guards with it. In the days leading up to the military taking over, the medics and EMTs had come under gunfire several times. One medic had been killed for allegedly taking too long to treat a gang member who also later died of a knife wound. The fire department wasn't faring much better. There were fires burning all over the city and the ladder and engine companies were doing their best to make sure no one was inside them and that the fires didn't spread, but they, too, had been shot at. Jason knew some of the firemen were now wearing bulletproof vests underneath their turnout coats.

As everyone prepared to head out, the rest of Jason's four-person team approached him. Fred Ingram and Reynaldo Escalera had been in his squad for the past several years, and they all worked well together. The fourth team member was Jason's partner, Nanette March. He'd been hesitant to trust a woman to cover his six when she'd first been assigned to him four years ago, even though she had served eight years in the Marines before being hired by the NYPD. While there were many female officers in his precinct, that had been the first time he'd been partnered with one. But those doubts had been eradicated after she'd single-handedly taken down a gang member who had swung at Jason with a baseball bat while the partners were wrestling with another suspect. Jason had just been able to avoid being cracked over the head before Nan had kicked some serious ass. By the time their backup arrived, the two officers had already cuffed and planted both suspects into the back of their patrol car. All four involved had survived with non-life threatening injuries, but if that happened again tonight, two would be dead without a second thought, and he'd be damned if it was going to be Nan and him.

He knew his partner had been under a lot of stress lately, as were many other men and women around the city. It went beyond the disbandment and general hatred of the police department. Some members of the NYPD had been branded traitors by people of their own race. Two months ago, at a supposedly peaceful protest, a self-righteous and pious black woman had spit in Nan's face, calling her a disgrace to her heritage. All because the woman stood on one side of the Thin Blue Line and Nan stood on the other. It didn't matter how many lives she'd saved over the years. Or how many children and adults she'd shielded from the horrors of life. Or the fact she'd managed to make them smile or offer a comforting shoulder when they'd been having one of the worst days of their lives. She was still being called a disgraced traitor.

But Nan had stood tall and proud, and swore to protect the very people who thought she was the scum of the earth. Irony was a bitch at times.

"Everyone ready?" Jason asked. While they had all been the same rank, he was the one with the most seniority, so the others tended to look up to him.

Ingram cracked his knuckles. "Let's do this."

On the way to the door, Jason did a mental check of his equipment one more time. Black clothing. Black tactical gloves. Bulletproof vest. A 9mm handgun on his right hip with a 380 backup piece on his ankle. Extra clips of ammo for both. Ka-Bar knife at his waist in the back. Taser, Pepper spray. Night vision googles, Maglite, and two pairs of handcuffs hanging on his left hip. Zip ties in one of the cargo pants pockets. A black ski mask in another one. Communications piece in his ear with a mic attached to his shirt collar. Cell phone. It wasn't much different than what he'd carried on a normal shift, but for some reason it weighed heavier, probably a trick of his mind.

He was as prepared for what they were about to do as the rest of his team was. They hit the alleyway, and after making sure things were clear, he led them out to the street. Keeping to the shadows, they made their way to the stairs leading to one of the many subway stations throughout the city. The trains had been shut down at 9:30 p.m.—a half hour before the curfew went into effect. The teams of police officers turned vigilantes would be able to use the track tunnels to get around easier without being spotted. At least, until 5:30 in the morning, when mass transit started up again.

Jumping a turnstile, they scanned the area. A few homeless people were scattered about, seeking warmth from the dropping temperatures outside. While the first two weeks of the ninth month had been above normal in the heat index, two days ago, a cold front had swooped down from Canada. The overnight temps had plunged from the low seventies to the high fifties. Thank God for small favors since it meant they wouldn't been sweating to death in their long-sleeved shirts and heavy boots.

"How're Amy and Joey?" Nan asked Jason as they walked side-by-side down the dimly lit tracks, avoiding the third rail.

He shrugged. "Spoke to Amy about an hour ago. They made it to her parents' farm upstate without a problem other than traffic. Everyone who can is fleeing the cities."

The only reason he hadn't taken them himself then returned to meet the rest of the cops was that his brother-in-law was taking his own wife and kids to the family home and offered to take Amy and Joey. Amy's brother, Adam Sheffield, was a retired Green Beret and Jason trusted him with his family's lives. Between Adam and Mr. Sheffield, who had an arsenal of weapons and ammunition he'd been stockpiling the past few months, Jason was sure they were all safe for now. It also helped that the riots and rampant criminal activity were mainly restricted to the cities, even though in some areas it had spread, but who knew how long that would last.

"Smart thing to do. Unfortunately there are millions of people with no alternative places to go."

"And that's why we're doing what we're doing. How are your folks?"

Nan had been born and raised in Pelham, just north of the city. "I tried to get them to go stay with my uncle, but Dad refuses to leave. He and few neighbors set up a watch to defend their homes. Mom wouldn't leave without him."

That was the dilemma many people faced in the city and the closest suburbs. To leave was to basically say goodbye to anything they couldn't take with them. Criminals and delinquents were going to have field days with looting and vandalism.

The sound of running feet had all four drawing their weapons and fading into the shadows. From the sound of it, there were several people coming down the tracks. Young voices and laughter echoed off the walls, getting louder by the moment. Dumb, fucking kids and their damn parents for letting them out after curfew. Clearly they hadn't listened to the warnings on every news channel and radio station. They'd be lucky to get home alive.

Half a dozen teenage boys and girls ran past the team, completely oblivious to their presence. Any other night, the three men and one woman would have stopped the teens, frisked them for weapons and drugs, then either told them to get the fuck home or arrested them. But that was no longer on their agenda. The teens were on their own, as long as they weren't in any immediate danger. Jason just hoped they weren't more stupid than they appeared and wouldn't get into more trouble than they could handle.

Once the reckless group was out of sight, the team started their journey again. The rats, cockroaches, and a few more homeless people were the only other living things they came across by the time they arrived at their intended station and

SCATTERED MOMENTS IN TIME

headed for the stairs. Back up on street level, they ducked into an alley. There were still a few cars driving around the city and even fewer pedestrians hurrying to wherever they were going. Sirens from fire engines and ambulances wailed in the distance, mixing with car alarms going off, and radios and TVs blaring through open windows.

The roadblocks hadn't made it to this part of the city yet, but they would be there soon. The only people who were allowed to be out after curfew were those whose jobs were vital. Doctors, nurses, EMTs, 911 dispatchers, and the like had needed to apply for curfew exclusions prior to yesterday with evidence confirming their identity and profession. While the 911 system was still up and running, all calls were being fielded by the USARNG, which meant many of them were being ignored. Only calls about life and death situations were being responded to. For everything else, the victims of crimes were on their own.

Jason turned to his teammates. "Nan and I will take this side of the street, you two take the other side. Check any open doors, the stairwells, alleys, and rooftops. Stay in contact with us at all times. If you need to check something out, let us know, and we'll cover your six. Remember, the rules of engagement and use of deadly force no longer apply. Felony in progress with a victim, shoot to kill no matter what. Our mission is simple—protect and save the innocent and stay alive to return to our families in the morning."

The others nodded and then Ingram and Escalera ran across the street, disappearing into the shadows. With most of the street lights shot out, and lights off or dimmed in most of the businesses and apartments, there was plenty of darkness to hide in. It was both an advantage and curse for the team.

An hour passed and they had checked the buildings covering only two of the four block radius they'd been assigned to. When they were done, they'd start all over again until dawn. They'd come across many people who hadn't been able to leave. The elderly and families with small children with nowhere to go broke Jason's heart. There was nothing he or the others could do for them, but suggest things to keep them safe. They'd managed to convince several people to join forces and blockade themselves in one apartment. The more people fighting and surviving together, the better chances they had.

Across the city, hundreds of former police officers, separated into four person teams, were doing exactly what this one was doing—but some hadn't been as lucky with their sectors. There had been a shitload of activity over the airwaves, including several gunfights. Two 10-13s had been called, which was the radio code for an officer down, but they'd been on the other side of the city so Jason's team had been unable to respond.

The USARNG had rolled into the neighborhood about twenty minutes ago and began setting up on the corners, blocking the streets. Many NYPD officers had served in the military, and through the grapevine, they'd come up with hand signals that allowed them to walk the streets without being stopped by the guardsmen. It was one less thing they had to worry about. The USARNG knew they were assigned to a losing battle and were willing to covertly join forces with the new vigilantes to try and save the city. They were far outnumbered and needed all the help they could get. Anarchy was raising its ugly head and it wasn't a pretty sight.

Gang members were trying to take over the streets and gunfire filled the air. But still, Jason and his team forged on. An explosion from a thrown Molotov cocktail ignited a store two blocks down and shook the ground. They could feel the flash of unbearable heat despite the distance. People screamed and scrambled down the fire escapes. Jason and Nan started to run in that direction to rescue those they could when a closer scream stopped them cold.

"Help! Rape! Someone please help me!"

Gunfire followed. *Fuck!*

The guardsmen would have to help those escaping the fire. Looking up, Jason tried to determine which building the pleas and shots had come from. Ingram and Escalera came running from across the street, pointing to the building on Jason and Nan's left.

"Up there!" Ingram shouted over the commotion from two blocks down. "Think they're on the roof!"

Finding the door to the building locked, Jason pulled out his heavy Maglite and swung it at the glass panel in the door. It shattered but the wire mesh insert held fast. Damn, where was ESU with a battering ram when you needed one? Oh, yeah, the Emergency Services Unit had been disbanded along with the rest of them.

Escalera pushed Jason out of the way and tackled the wire with a cutter he must have added to his supply of tools and weapons. It took longer than desired, but soon a hole was big enough for Nan to get her smaller hand through to unlock the door. There were two sets of stairs in this building. One just inside the doorway and another at the far end of a long hallway. There was an elevator, but with random power outages and people setting buildings on fire, none of them felt like getting trapped in one.

Jason signaled for Ingram and Escalera to take the stairs at the other end of the hall, while he and Nan started up the closer one. Darkness quickly enveloped them. The lights in the stairwell were all out. Instead of using flashlights, they first donned their ski masks and then the night vision goggles. The masks were to protect their identities if any shit went down, which was a given at this point. It was six flights of stairs to get to the roof, but that was something they had done many times in the past. Their surroundings were a sickly green color through their goggles, and Jason had a flash sense of playing some moronic video game. What he wouldn't give for that to be true.

Aside from the sounds of TVs, radios, a baby crying, and some pots and pans rattling, there wasn't any other activity as they passed each floor. When they reached the door to the roof, Jason pulled off his night vision goggles and let his eyes adjust for a moment. Pushing the door open a crack, the woman's screams and crying filled the air, mixed with the drunken laughter of several men.

Up here on the roof, the moonlight made it easier to see, and Jason signaled for Nan to remove hers. While they were an advantage in the pitch-black darkness, they were a hindrance in lighter areas. Both slipped out the door into the shadows with weapons drawn. Huge, silent air conditioning units and a utility shack gave them plenty of cover, but also blocked their view of the situation.

Creeping forward, Jason took the lead, confident Nan had his back. A glass vodka bottle was thrown into the air and someone picked it off with a bullet, shattering it. So much for hoping they were too drunk to shoot straight.

Peeking around one of the air conditioning units, Jason spotted six men in their late teens and early twenties, dressed in either black or denim jeans, hanging well below their hips. Shirts, bandanas, and hats in blue identified them as belonging to one of the many gangs that fought to rule the streets. Beer and alcohol bottles were strewn all over the place as the men partied. The smell of urine and pot permeated the night air, blending with the smoke from the fire a few blocks away, which had spread to the upper floors. The gang members were laughing and watching it burn. Two of them, Jason realized, had been arrested by him and Nan before on drug and weapons charges. Huddled against a waist-high wall at the edge of the building was a disheveled, nearly naked woman trying to cover herself up with her torn clothes. She attempted to crawl away from the men who had clearly raped and assaulted her, but one of them blocked her route and pointed his gun at her. "Where do ya think you're going, slut?" He grabbed his crotch and leered at her.

"We're not done with you yet. This fucking party is just getting started."

She was dirty, trembling, and crying. Her lips were split and bleeding, and one eye was bruised and swollen shut, but that didn't stop Jason from recognizing her. One of the most vocal leaders, she'd helped organize many of the protests throughout the city, and had been on TV many times calling for the president to disband the police forces. Irony was being a real bitch tonight.

While the women had been completely against the police officers, there was no way Jason's team was abandoning her now. They'd sworn to protect the innocent, and tonight, whether they liked it or not, she was an innocent.

Giving Nan hand signals, he told her how many perpetrators there were and for her to move behind another air conditioning unit so they could engage. Ingram's voice came over his headset. "Delta 3-3 and 3-4 in position."

Jason ducked back and spoke into his mic as softly as he could. "Delta 3-3 take out bandana around neck. Delta 3-4 take out vodka. Delta 3-2 sunglasses. I've got the babysitter. If you have a shot after that, take out the other two. On the count of three."

If all went well, the gang of six would be down to two in less than five seconds. Aiming his gun, Jason leaned out from behind the cover just enough to get a bead on his target. In a hushed voice, he counted, "One . . . two . . . three."

The four deafening reports were almost simultaneous and the targets' bodies jerked as they were hit in either the chest or the back by the bullets they deserved. One of gangbangers squeezed off a round as his hand involuntarily jerked the trigger of his gun before he fell into a heap on the ground. The other two shouted and dove for cover, firing their weapons at the unknown assailants who had interrupted their party. The woman screamed, unsure of what was happening.

"Fuck!" Escalera spat into his mic. "I'm hit."

"He'll live," his partner added immediately. "Took it in the arm. Damn, can't get a shot at these two fuckers."

One of the two ducked his head out, not knowing he was caught in the middle of the four people who wanted to send him to hell. Nan fired without hesitation and the bullet went in one temple and out the other, killing him instantly.

Suddenly, several shots were fired at once, but not at the team. The woman, who had minutes ago been a victim, had picked up one of the dead men's guns and kept firing into the last man standing until there were no bullets left and his body lay in a pool of blood.

Jason stepped forward as the woman continued to squeeze the now useless trigger. The *click, click, click* was barely audible over the ringing in his ears. Nan appeared beside him, her gun holstered, and in her hand was a ratty blanket she'd found. She slowly approached the woman who burst into tears again while screaming her rage at the dead men. Nan took the harmless gun and tried to calm her. "*Shhh.* You're going to be okay. We're here to help. That's all."

The screams of fury turned into wails of grief and who knew what else she was feeling. The woman allowed Nan to cover her with the blanket as she rocked back and forth pulling it around her for warmth and security. Ingram and Escalera appeared with the latter holding his blood-soaked, injured arm. It didn't look too bad but a trip to their underground medical station was in order. They couldn't risk going to a hospital ER unless it was a dire situation

The woman's heartbreaking sobs and tears ebbed as she looked at the dead men and then up at her rescuers. Her eyes widened as she suddenly noticed the ski masks covering their faces. "Wh-who are you?"

Jason's gaze met those of his teammates before turning back to the woman and saying what he knew they all felt. "We are the future.

48

PART FOUR

I AM

I am a number, carved in metal and pinned on my chest.

I am one of the dutiful who work 24/7/365, missing holidays and important moments in my family's lives.

I am one of a handful of family members who followed in my grandfather's footsteps.

I am one of few childhood friends who chose the same career path.

I am one of a group who trained, studied, and sweat together.

I am one of the proud who swore to uphold the laws of the land, help those in need, and protect others from danger.

I am one of the loyal who defends those same laws whether or not I agree with them.

I am one of the honored who wears my country's flag on my

sleeve, knowing one day that same flag will be draped over my coffin.

I am one of the masses who call each other brothers and sisters, not of blood, but of the heart.

I am one of the feared, by those who choose to do harm to their fellow man.

I am one of the respected, by those who understand how hard I work to keep them safe.

I am one of the envied who can honestly say "I love my job."

I am one of the despised because of the extremely small percent who damaged the public's trust.

I am one of the misunderstood, by those who have never walked in my boots.

I am one of the hated, by those with narrow minds, little conscience, few morals, and who think the laws do not pertain to them.

I am one of those who are looked upon with awe by children who want to grow up to be like me.

I am one of the brave who run into danger while others run away.

I am one drop in a sea of blue that spans the farthest corners of the earth.

I am one of the thousands that walk the thin blue line knowing every day may be the one I don't go home to my loved ones.

I am one of the heartbroken who stand shoulder to shoulder, saluting the fallen while trying to hold back my tears.

I am one of the saddened who either took a life or could not save one despite every effort.

I am one of the mourned who died defending the rights and lives of people I never knew.

I am one of the remembered, my name etched in stone with those who went before me.

I am a Police Officer.

PART FIVE

STOKE THE FLAMES

To my Uncle Jerry, the fireman of the family.
Not a day goes by that I don't think of you and all the wonderful, funny times we shared.

CHAPTER ONE

"*I* brought you a present!"

Jenna Anderson groaned at the sound of her best friend's voice. She loved Caroline Wagner dearly, but her friend was always bringing her little presents, usually with hunky men on them, that she didn't need or want. Last time, it was a mouse pad with a bare-chested surfer on it. Not that Jenna had anything against hunky men, it was just men like that never took an interest in her. Over the years, she had dated quite a few men that piqued her interest intellectually, but while she liked their personalities, she never found herself interested in them romantically. She'd tried to develop a physical connection with some of them but found the sex unfulfilling, and she refused to settle for just half a satisfying relationship.

"I'm afraid to ask," she said without looking up from correcting her third-grade students' math tests.

"But this was for a good cause." Caroline tossed a large, thin booklet on top of the papers her friend was grading.

"*The Hannaford, PA, Fire Department Calendar,*" Jenna read. The glossy cover photo was of twelve gorgeous firemen standing in front of a bright red fire truck wearing the pants of their fire gear, boots, and helmets and nothing else. Their bulging biceps and chest muscles, along with their flat six-packs, had been oiled to show every luscious detail. "A good cause, huh?"

"Yup," Caroline replied as she sat on the edge of Jenna's desk. "The money goes to help the families of firemen that died in the line of duty. Check out Mr. October. Yummy!"

Jenna tossed the unopened calendar to the side. "Why look at what I can't have?"

"Come on, Jenna. You can have any man you set your mind on. You're pretty, smart, and fun to be with. You just have to learn how to flirt better." She leaned over and tugged on the front of Jenna's blouse and added, "And show off a little more cleavage now and then."

"I teach third grade. I think showing off my cleavage is against the law."

"Not here silly. I've got an idea. You and I are going out this Saturday night, but I get to pick out what you wear. Deal?" She hopped off the desk and stood before Jenna with her hands on her hips, eyebrows raised.

Gaping, Jenna narrowed her eyes. "Deal? What do I get out of it?"

"If you're lucky, a hot night of sex!" Waving goodbye, Caroline ran out of the classroom before her friend could refuse.

Jenna stared at her friend's retreating form. Didn't she get it? Caroline was a tall, willowy blonde with a body men drooled over. Jenna on the other hand was five-foot-five and twenty pounds heavier than she wanted to be. She would sometimes joke that her curves had curves, yet the extra weight bothered her. With mousy brown hair and eyes to match, she knew she would never win any beauty contests. She often wondered how she and Caroline remained such good friends all these years.

They had first met in high school, then ended up as college roommates at Penn State. After graduation, they'd both returned to their hometown and were hired as teachers at the same school.

Caroline taught fourth grade. Aside from their chosen careers, the two had very little in common. Caroline was outgoing and could talk to anyone; Jenna was more of a homebody, quieter and far from the social butterfly her friend was. Yet their friendship saw them through the best and worst times of their lives. Jenna had been there for her friend when Caroline's parents died in their home, due to an undetected carbon monoxide leak, five months after the women graduated college. Then Caroline had taken care of Jenna as she recovered from an emergency appendectomy last summer. They were much more than friends. They were family.

Glancing at her watch, Jenna was amazed to see it was five-thirty already. She needed to head home to feed her dog and then do some laundry. Packing the pile of test papers and the children's English essays into her tote bag, she noticed the beefcake calendar still on her desk. Not wanting her students to see it, she added it to the soft, leather attaché. Putting on her raincoat, she grabbed her purse and tote bag and locked the classroom door as she left.

The rainstorm that had pounded the area earlier had finally died down, leaving some mild flooding in the streets. Jenna's small house was only ten blocks from the school, and although it took her a few minutes longer than usual, she got home safely.

Stepping out of her Altima, she heard Dudley, her border collie mix, barking like crazy in the fenced-in backyard. The canine was able to go in and out of the house through a doggie-door Jenna had installed for him. This way if she was late for some reason, Dudley would be able to go outside to do his business. Thankfully, he only barked when she pulled up or when a squirrel dared to enter his domain.

Jenna unlocked the front door and entered to find the overly-friendly ball of fur already in the kitchen waiting for her, his food bowl in his mouth. She put her bags on the kitchen table and took off her coat, all while grinning at him. "Let me guess, you're hungry?"

Dudley pranced over and dropped the plastic dish at her feet. Laughing, Jenna picked it up and went to the pantry to fill it with kibble. After putting the chock-full bowl in the corner of the kitchen, she grabbed the dog's water dish and topped it off too.

Once Dudley was taken care of, Jenna opened the freezer and looked over the array of frozen meals. They all appeared boring, so she grabbed one at random and popped it into the microwave. It wasn't that she didn't like to cook, she just didn't like to cook for one person. It reminded her she was alone. Maybe Caroline was right. Maybe she did need a night out on the town looking for a single guy.

While her dinner heated up, Jenna began to empty the paperwork from her tote bag. She wanted to get everything graded before her Tuesday-night TV entertainment came on. She was a fan of America's Got Talent and was looking forward to watching it with a pint of mint chocolate chip ice cream. *No wonder I can't lose weight*, she thought wryly.

As she pulled out the last of her students' essays, the calendar fell out onto the table. Putting the papers down, she picked up the booklet and leafed through it. Just because she couldn't attract any guy this hot, didn't mean she couldn't drool in secret. Flipping through the pages, she suddenly stopped at October. *Holy cow!* Caroline hadn't been kidding; Mr. October was downright sinful. Black hair, startling blue eyes, and his five o'clock shadow were just the beginning. His broad shoulders and chiseled chest were enough to make her feel heat radiating from her core. She ran her finger down the man's trim waist and stopped at the top of the navy-blue work pants he'd posed in. A thin coating of dark hair traveled from his chest downward, disappearing under his belt. Jenna's eyes traveled back up the enticing photo and found a hint of mischief in the man's eyes and smile as he leaned against the garage door jamb of a firehouse with the red trucks in the background. His arms were crossed, causing his biceps to bulge and Jenna's mouth to water.

Now why couldn't she meet a man like this? Oh, well, she thought, he's probably dumb as rocks and has no personality. Tossing the calendar onto a stack of magazines, she brought herself back to reality. Grading papers, a cardboard dinner, and a night of watching TV—alone.

CHAPTER TWO

*S*ighing to herself, Jenna handed back her students' math tests. Everyone had passed except Christopher Fallon. This was the second test he'd failed this semester, and if he didn't pass the next two tests and the final exam, he'd wind up in summer school or being held back a grade. The last two tests had been sent home to be signed by his guardian. It was well known that the boy's parents had been killed in a car accident the year before. Chris had been the lone survivor of the crash and had miraculously only suffered minor injuries. He was now being raised by his uncle and grandmother. Jenna had met Chris's grandmother, Therese Fallon, at the school's parent/teacher night. She vaguely recalled that the uncle had been unable to attend due to work, although she couldn't recall what he did for a living.

Jenna handed Chris his folded test so no one else would see his grade and the request for a meeting with his uncle. She noticed he didn't look at the paper before stuffing into the knapsack he kept under his desk. He might not be a straight-A student, but he was doing well in all his other subjects. Hopefully, with a little help, he could improve his math grade enough to pass. He was one of her favorite students. Despite his loss, he was still a delightful boy who was popular with the other students. She could imagine him in ten years—the girls his age would be flocking to him like moths to a flame.

A short while later, as Jenna was teaching her students about the Pilgrims and Plymouth Rock, the fire alarm resounded throughout the school. Knowing it wasn't a drill—she would have been notified prior to the alarm—she calmly had her class line up at the door before instructing them to walk out to their designated meeting area. They'd practiced fire drills every other week to ensure the students knew what was expected of them and where to go. Unfortunately, in this day and age, they also practiced active-shooter drills too, although they called them "code red" alerts so as to not frighten the children.

Jenna grabbed her student roster, and after making sure no one was left in the room, she closed the door behind her. Her students walked single file out to the playground. She did a headcount, consulting her roster and laying her eyes on each child, as they stopped at their assigned spot. All were present and accounted for.

Spotting Caroline and her charges, Jenna eased her way through the crowd of children, while keeping an eye on her own students. "What's going on? Who pulled the alarm?"

"I don't know," Caroline replied, shaking her head. "My kids were in the middle of a science quiz." She turned to her students and reminded them not to talk about the questions on the test.

Jenna's next thought was interrupted by the sounds of sirens as several fire trucks and a police car drove up to the school with their emergency lights blazing to the delight of the students. They all watched in awe as several firemen climbed off the trucks, grabbed pieces of equipment, and entered the building. The school principal, Jeff Carpenter, was at the front of the school talking with the fire chief. It appeared to be a false alarm but would take several minutes before they confirmed it.

Suddenly aware a few of her students were horsing around, Jenna interrupted the impending chaos and calmed them down. Five minutes later, the firemen filed out of the school and apparently gave the all clear signal to the principal, who then waved for the teachers and students to return to their classrooms. As Jenna marched her students past the big trucks, Chris pointed to the group of firemen who had taken off their helmets and turnout coats. "There's my Uncle Cade!"

Before she could stop the boy, he was running toward the firemen. Seeing the principal's secretary standing nearby, Jenna caught her attention. "Diane, can you take my class back inside for me, please? I need to speak to Chris's uncle for a moment."

"No problem," the woman answered.

Jenna followed her wayward student and spotted Chris next to a tall fireman who was standing with his back to her. His broad shoulders were evident under his navy-blue T-shirt, which also showcased his trim waist. The rest of him was covered beneath his turnout pants and boots. When she reached them, Jenna spoke loudly to be heard over the idling fire truck engines, "Excuse me, Mr. Fallon?"

The man turned around to face her, and Jenna lost all train of thought as she stared into the bluest eyes she'd ever seen. *Oh. My. God! Christopher Fallon's uncle is Mr. October!*

"Yes?"

His rich, deep, baritone voice sent chills through her spine, and Jenna couldn't wait to hear him say more than one word. She was relieved when her student spoke up since she could no longer remember what she wanted to say. "Ms. Anderson, this is my Uncle Cade. He's a fireman!"

Cade chuckled at his eight-year-old nephew and his grin was punctuated by two adorable dimples. "I think Ms. Anderson figured that out on her own, kiddo. I'm sure the uniform and the big, red truck had something to do with it."

Jenna realized she was staring and mentally shook herself. "Um, hello. I'm Chris's teacher, Jenna Anderson."

"Hi, Cade Fallon. It's nice to meet you." He held out his hand, and Jenna's skin tingled when she shook it.

"Can I see you?" She immediately blushed at how that sounded. "I . . . I mean to discuss Chris. I was sending a note home with him."

His eyes narrowed. "Everything all right?"

After glancing down and seeing Chris was busy watching the firemen stow their gear back on the truck, Jenna returned her gaze to Cade's. "It's about his math grades; they're not improving. I was hoping we could sit down and discuss it."

"Uh, sure," he answered, then gestured to the activity behind him. "Obviously I can't right now, and I don't get off shift until seven tonight."

"What about tomorrow morning at seven before the students arrive? We can talk in my classroom."

"Tomorrow morning's fine. Which room is yours?"

"Hey, Fallon! Let's go!"

Cade waved at another fireman who was climbing into the front passenger seat of the truck. "Be right there, Chief!" He turned back to Jenna and raised his eyebrows, looking for an answer to his question.

Jenna almost got lost in his blue eyes again. "Uh, the hall monitor will be in the lobby by then. Just ask her for directions."

"Great. Um, I gotta go. I'll see you in the morning." He squatted next to his nephew. "I'll see you tonight, squirt."

"Will you wake me up if you get a late call?" Chris asked, his eyes filled with hope.

His uncle shook his head. "Sorry, you know the rules—not on a school night. But I'm first on the list to be relieved tonight, so I should be home on time, okay?"

"Okay." Chris gave his uncle a quick hug before the man stood back up.

Jenna rested her hand on her student's shoulder. "Come on, Chris. We have to get back to class and your uncle has to go back to work."

"Bye, Uncle Cade."

"I'll see you later, kiddo." Addressing Jenna, he added, "And I'll see you in the morning."

Jenna shivered at the thought of seeing Cade Fallon again.

CHAPTER THREE

*A*s the fire engine pulled away, Cade's attention fell on his nephew and the pretty teacher walking back into the school. He suddenly regretted sending his mother to the parent/teacher conferences this year, since all of them had fallen on nights he'd had to work. He would've liked to have met Ms. Jenna Anderson before today. Her warm brown eyes had almost matched her chestnut-colored hair which framed her heart-shaped face. He hadn't missed the blush that had stolen across her face when she'd asked if she could see him before recovering and clarifying what she'd meant.

Over the past few weeks, he'd gotten more attention from the opposite sex than he'd ever imagined after the release of the new fire department's fundraiser calendar. Thanks to a bet he'd lost on a Phillies' baseball game, he'd ending up posing for this year's edition along with eleven other firemen. The guys who'd been in last year's calendar had tried to warn the newbies that some of the female fans could get out of hand, but Cade and the others hadn't realized how much of an understatement that'd been. Not only had there been a huge turnout for them to sign the calendars at a local bookstore, but women had been stopping by the firehouse for autographs and pictures. It wasn't long before Cade was being stopped at the supermarket, gas stations, on his runs through the park, and even at fire scenes by his "adoring fans" as the chief called them. Those two words were usually followed by an eye roll from both Chief Kellum and Cade. The attention had gotten old very quickly.

Cade's coworkers were enjoying the rewards of having a "celebrity" in their squad, though, since many of the women brought baked goods on their trips to the station, as if that would entice "Mr. October" into asking them out. Ten years ago, Cade would've taken advantage of his notoriety in a heartbeat, but those days were gone. Not only had the appeal of dating almost any women he'd asked out fizzled, but he now had a responsibility of raising an eight-year-old boy who thought his uncle/godfather walked on water.

What was supposed to be a family trip to a Chuck E. Cheese for dinner one night, had turned into a disaster that destroyed them. A teenager texting on his phone, instead of watching where the 4000-pound vehicle he'd been driving was going, ran a stop sign and T-boned the Fallon's minivan. Caleb, Cade's older brother, who'd been at the wheel, had been killed instantly, when the other vehicle slammed into his door. The impact sent the minivan careening into a telephone pole on the opposite side. Caleb's wife, Irene, who'd been sitting in the front passenger seat, died several hours later in surgery. Miraculously, young Christopher had survived in his rear booster seat, with minor injuries. The first six months following the accident, the boy had suffered from night terrors, reliving the tragedy that'd taken his parents from him, but with the help of a therapist, he was now sleeping through the night again.

In the blink of an eye, Cade had gone from being a carefree uncle, to a mature father-figure. Gone were his nights of carousing bars with his other single friends, looking for a woman interested in a little fun with no commitments. Maybe that was why having all those women throw themselves at him because of the calendar was bothering him. Any relationship he found himself in now, whether brief or long-term, he'd have to take into consideration his responsibility to Chris. Cade couldn't have a string of one or two-night stands revolving through his front door. Having his mother living in the small apartment attached to his house didn't help either—at least when it came to relationships. His mother had been amazing helping Cade with Chris and he couldn't have done it without her. While he'd known he would become his nephew's guardian if anything happened to both Caleb and Irene, Cade had never expected to have to follow through with it. Irene's sister was Chris's godmother, but her career traveling the world as an archaeologist with her own cable television show wasn't conducive to raising a child. Iris called whenever she could, emailed often, and visited when she was stateside, but the thirty-year-old would've had to give up her career and settle down if she'd been named Chris's guardian. Cade, on the other hand, had a stable job with no traveling, owned a home, and had the support of family and friends.

"Hey, Fallon! One of your adoring fans awaits!"

Cade rolled his eyes after glancing in the direction Mason Garrett was pointing. The bastard was chuckling at the woman standing near the overhead garage door to the fire station that was in the process of rolling upward. Brooke Hanson was a two-time divorcée who'd been stopping by at least once a week with baked goods she'd probably purchased at a local store before putting them on a tray to appear as if she'd made them. It was clear to every guy at the station that the forty-plus year old had an intimate relationship with a plastic surgeon—a few lifts here, a few tucks there, and boom, a Barbie-wanna-be. While she was attractive in her own way, she did nothing for Cade. He preferred women who were comfortable in their own skin—someone natural, like Jenna Anderson. And damn, the thought of the curvy teacher had his cock twitching in his pants. He hoped he didn't embarrass himself by getting hard during their meeting tomorrow.

Sighing, Cade jumped off the truck and wracked his brain for a way to get rid of Brooke quickly, as he blocked traffic for the fire truck to swing out into the street before backing into the bay. Unfortunately, nothing he'd tried before had worked.

"Mr. October is Chris Fallon's uncle?" Caroline squealed while sitting on the edge of Jenna's desk. "Oh. My. God! How incredibly cool is that? I may have to come in early tomorrow just to check him out in person. Is he as hot as his picture?"

"Hotter," Jenna murmured into the hands she held over her face, after the last of her students had left for the day.

"Did you flirt with him, at least?"

Her gaze flew to her friend's face in amazement. "In front of his nephew, my student? Are you nuts?"

Huffing, Caroline rolled her eyes. "I would have definitely been undressing him with my eyes."

Jenna didn't want to admit she had been doing just that in her mind as she'd been talking to Cade Fallon. The man was even better looking in person, and his voice was like honey. She still could remember how it had flowed through her, straight to her core. She could only imagine what he sounded like when he was trying to seduce a woman—although he probably didn't have to try hard. Not with those good looks.

Standing, she gathered up the student's book reports to take home. "And don't even think of showing up and being a peeping Thomasina in the morning. It's a parent/teacher conference. Nothing more."

"It could be."

Jenna narrowed her eyes. "No, it can't be. Chris is my student."

"Only for six more weeks. Then he's my student." Caroline frowned. "Well, damn. If you strike out, I have to wait a whole year before I can hit on him."

"I'm not going to strike out, because I'm not going to hit on him. Now, knock it off. This is a meeting because my student is failing math, not so I can get a date. And I highly doubt I'm his type."

Her friend's frown became more pronounced. "What does that mean?"

Letting out an exasperated sigh, Jenna grabbed her tote bag, purse, and insulated lunch bag and started for the door. "It means I'm short, fat, and dumpy. I'd give anything to look like you."

"Jenna Marie Anderson!"

Pulling up short, she spun around at her barked full name to find Caroline glaring at her. Anger filled her friend's eyes as she stood tall with her arms across her chest. "Are you out of your mind? Is that what you think you look like? Short, fat, and dumpy? I don't believe you." She smirked. "Well, I do about the short part, but almost all my friends are shorter than me. But fat and dumpy are never words I'd use to describe you."

"Of course you wouldn't because you're my friend. Friends are supposed to lie to make you feel good."

"No. Friends are supposed to tell you the truth enough times until you finally believe what they're telling you." Her eyes filling up with tears that didn't spill over, Caroline stepped closer and brushed her hand down Jenna's cheek. "You really don't know how pretty you are, do you? I wish I had your curves. And you're so not dumpy, my friend. Your eyes are so expressive, especially when you laugh. Your hair is thick and gorgeous. Mine takes an hour and six products every morning to straighten the kinks out of it, and then I pray it doesn't frizz the moment I step out of the house. When we go out, you get just as many guys checking you out as I do, if not more. It all depends on what they're looking for. If it's a party girl, it's me they're eyeing. If it's someone they can take home to meet their mother and maybe have a long-term relationship with, it's you they want."

Although Caroline believed the words she'd said, Jenna couldn't. But she didn't want her best friend to know that, so she smiled and said, "Then I better go shopping because I don't have a thing to wear if I have to meet some guy's mother."

"Now you're talking. Let's head to Kohl's; I'm always lucky there. Let's find something that'll knock Mr. October's socks off —among other things—when you see him in the morning."

Rolling her eyes, Jenna followed Caroline out the door. *Talk about one-track minds.*

CHAPTER FOUR

*C*ade was grateful Chris's teacher had an adult-sized chair next to her desk for him to sit in since there was no way he'd fit in any of the students' tiny chairs lined up throughout the classroom. Ms. Anderson had put a lot of time into decorating the room to make it both appealing and educational for her students, but she was the only thing holding Cade's attention. Yesterday, she'd been wearing black slacks, comfortable flats, and burgundy blouse covered by a lightweight, black blazer. It had been a bit plain, and purely professional, and had hidden most of her curves, which were much more apparent today The black, white, and emerald green, geometric print dress she had on was knocking his socks off, and he was finding it difficult to keep his gaze on her face and not the V-neck of the garment. It wasn't inappropriate at all, but for a heterosexual man who found her attractive, it definitely had him thinking impure thoughts. She'd probably want to slap him if she knew how much he wished the V plunged another inch or two, enough to show him the creamy skin on the inside of both lush breasts. Her brown hair had soft waves, and Cade wanted to reach up and see if the strands were as silky as he thought they were. Her eyes were almost the same shade as her hair, but they were filled with amber specks that made them sparkle. Cade's gaze dropped to her mouth. While her makeup was subtle, there was a glossy sheen to her lips and it had him thinking about all the dirty, delicious things those lips could do to him. Of course, that lead to him thinking about all the dirty, delicious things he wanted to do to her.

"He really is a sweet boy, Mr. Fallon, and he's passing all the other subjects with A and B averages," she was saying. "But unless he can pass the next two tests and the final with Cs or better, he'll have to go through summer school or repeat the grade." The emotion in her eyes told him it would kill her to fail Chris—she really cared about her students, that was evident.

"We'd hired a tutor, but clearly it's not working out. And, honestly, this Common Core math confuses the hell out of me. It was still simple addition, subtraction, multiplication, and division when I was his age. He probably understands it better than I do at this point. I guess I'll have to find a new tutor who can catch him up; any recommendations you have would be appreciated. It was hard enough to find this last one. I interviewed five. Turned out three of them recognized me from the fire department's fundraiser calendar and figured out who I was from my email address on the tutor ad." Why he'd just thrown that information out there was beyond him. He didn't want Jenna to think he was an egotistical man-whore or something. While a faint pink tinged her cheeks, she didn't mention having seen the calendar to his relief.

Jenna pulled her upper lip in between her teeth as she thought for a moment. Her next words surprised him. "If you'd like, I could tutor Chris three afternoons a week until the final. I usually stay an hour after school lets out to grade tests or homework, so I don't have to take everything home with me."

"Really? Um . . . that would be great. Either my mother or I can come get him afterward." Although, he'd make every effort to be the one picking Chris up if that meant seeing Jenna on a regular basis. But he didn't want her to think he was taking advantage of her fondness for the young boy. "Of course, I'll pay you."

Holding up her left hand, which was devoid of any engagement or wedding rings, she shook her head. "No. I can't let you do that—"

"But—"

"It wouldn't look good. I mean, someone might think I was being paid to pass him, so I can't take any money from you—or anything else. I really want to help Chris—he's one of my all-time favorite students—so having him pass will be payment enough."

Cade could tell she wasn't just saying that, but, damn, if paying her was out, he assumed a date was too. *Shit.* He hadn't come here thinking about asking her out, but the longer he sat there, the more he wanted to get to know her better. Well, summer recess was only a few more weeks away, and as long as Chris moved up to the next grade, Ms. Jenna Anderson would no longer be his teacher, so Cade hoped that meant he could ask her out then. For now, he was grateful she was willing to help his nephew. "Okay. But if you're successful, which I'm confident you will be, I'd be happy to send a letter to the school board to let them know what a great teacher you are."

The smile that spread across her face was making things uncomfortable in his jeans again. "That would be very nice of you. Most people don't think of that. They only write to the board if something goes wrong."

"My mom wrote letters at the end of every year to our teachers. I think she was grateful they didn't suspend my brother more often." When Jenna arched an eyebrow at him, Cade chuckled. "He wasn't a bully or anything; just liked playing practical jokes that sometimes got out of hand. It still amazes me that he'd met a woman who not only put up with him but tamed him too. They were the perfect couple."

He hadn't expected the wistfulness that entered his tone, and Jenna hadn't missed it either. Her gaze gentled.

"I'm very sorry for your loss, Mr. Fallon—"

"Please, call me Cade. Every time I hear Mr. Fallon I want to look around for my dad even though it's been fifteen years since he died."

She nodded. "Okay, Cade. I don't know what I would do if I lost any of my brothers. They can be pains in the ass sometimes but we're all very close."

"Caleb and I were close too. And Irene was the best sister-in-law I could ask for." He paused a moment before continuing. "It's hard, you know? Not only trying to get past the grief of losing them, but I'm so afraid I'm going to screw up raising Chris. If it wasn't for my mom, things would be a lot worse."

Cade hadn't meant for the conversation to turn so personal, but the pretty teacher was easy to talk to. She didn't seem uncomfortable with his confession that he was scared. Surprising him, she reached over and laid her hand on his bare forearm which was draped across the edge of her desk. The jolt of electricity he felt at her touch almost had him groaning. Her palm and fingers were as soft as her spoken words. "You're doing a great job raising him from what I see. There were a few times earlier in the year when I could tell he was hurting from the loss, but for the most part, he's been very upbeat and a delight to have in my classroom. You're obviously doing something right."

Clearing his throat, his gaze dropped to the floor in mild embarrassment. "Um. Thanks."

"Just keep doing what you're doing and you'll both be fine."

When she pulled her hand away, he immediately missed its warmth. Somewhere outside the classroom, a door opened and the sounds of children talking and laughing signaled the start of the school day. When Jenna stood, Cade knew their meeting was over and followed suit, holding out his hand. "Thanks for offering to tutor Chris. When do you want to start? I'll make sure my mom or I are here to pick him up."

"We can start this afternoon, if that's okay." Jenna placed her hand in his. It wasn't one of those limp or overly delicate handshakes some women gave, but a firm one, and he didn't want to let go. Reluctantly, he did.

"Today is fine. It's my day off, so I'll swing by at, what? Four?" School let out at 2:50 p.m.

"Four is perfect. I'm sorry; I don't mean to rush you out, but my mini tornadoes will be flying in at any moment."

"Great, and no problem. I'll . . . um . . . see you later then." With a wave, he strode toward the door when it was the last thing he wanted to do. He wished he could sit at the back of the class and just watch her. Well, at least he could look forward to seeing her again in eight hours, but they were going to be the longest ones of his life.

CHAPTER FIVE

*I*t was hard to keep her mind on grading the test papers on her desk while Chris worked on the new math problems Jenna had given him. Last Friday, two weeks after she'd started tutoring him, he'd gotten a B-minus on the first test. There was one more test coming up this Friday, and it would be the last one before the final, two weeks from today. The one-on-one sessions were helping him concentrate more on the problems without any outside distractions, like his handsome Uncle Cade. Oh wait, Cade was only a distraction to Jenna.

There had only been one afternoon, a week ago, when Cade hadn't been able to pick Chris up after the tutoring sessions were over—he'd been at a four-alarm fire the department had been battling all day at an apartment complex. Thankfully, nobody—firemen or civilians—had been injured. Chris's grandmother had come instead, and the two women had chatted for over fifteen minutes about all sorts of things. Mrs. Fallon was as sweet and friendly as her son and grandson were.

All the other times, though, Cade had been the one walking into Jenna's classroom at 4:00 p.m. on the nose. And each time he did, her heart fluttered in her chest and it suddenly became warm in the air-conditioned room. Glancing at the clock, she saw she only had five more minutes before her body would get all tingly at the sight of the strong, virile man with the most beautiful blue eyes she'd ever seen.

A chair scraping across the floor brought Jenna out of her fantasy, and she saw Chris approach her desk.

"Here, Ms. Anderson. I think I got them right, but I'm not sure about the last one."

She took the paper from him. "Okay, let's take a look."

As she compared his solutions to the answer key, he stood by her elbow and watched. Realizing what he'd done wrong in the last problem, she pointed out where he'd made his mistake and then let him try to solve it again. This time, he got the right answer. A grin spread across his face in triumph. "I did it! I got them all right!"

"That's awesome, kiddo."

Both woman and child startled at the booming voice. Neither had noticed Cade appear in the doorway and lean against the jamb.

"Hi, Uncle Cade!"

The man strode into the room and held his hand up for his nephew. "High five. I knew you could do it."

Chris slapped Cade's hand. "Thanks to Ms. Anderson. She's the best teacher."

A blush stole across Jenna's cheeks. Not at her student's compliment, but at the playful wink his uncle gave her. "I totally agree. She's the best."

Tearing her gaze away from Cade's, Jenna busied herself by putting papers into her tote bag. If someone asked her what the papers were, though, she'd have no clue. She'd have to sort them out later, when her brain wasn't short-circuiting thanks to the hunk standing no more than two feet away from her.

"Would you . . . um . . ." When Cade paused, suddenly seeming flustered, Jenna looked at him, questioningly. "I mean, if you're finished gathering your stuff, Chris and I will walk you to your car. I heard on the police scanner there was a robbery at the convenience store a few blocks away about forty-five minutes ago and they're still looking for the suspect. We'll make sure you're safely on your way before we leave."

Robberies weren't common in their area, but they also weren't unheard of. She was grateful for Cade's offer since she hadn't even been aware of it. School had already let out, and no one was left in the main office, so if the police had called to lock them down, no one had been there to answer the phone. "Thanks, I appreciate it. I doubt the suspect is stupid enough to still be nearby, but you never know."

Strolling down the hallway, Jenna listened as Chris told his uncle about the food fight that had taken place in the lunchroom earlier in the day. Four fifth graders had gotten three days of detention starting tomorrow for instigating it. Exiting the school, they turned right toward the parking lot, and Jenna inhaled deeply. It had been a beautiful day, and after a week of rainy or overcast days, the flower beds were in full bloom. But over their scent, a spicy masculine one tickled her nose and made her all too aware of how close Cade was walking beside her. Unfortunately, they reached her Altima far too quickly for her liking. When she unlocked it with the key fob, Cade opened the driver's door for her. It was such a gentlemanly gesture—one she hadn't experienced in quite a while—and she felt her heart flutter again. "Thank you."

"My pleasure."

The unexpected huskiness of his tone had her gaze slamming into his, and she was shocked to see what appeared to be desire there. It froze her into place—half in, half out of her car.

"Uncle Cade. Can you unlock my door?"

Chris's innocent request from several parking spaces over broke the spell between the two, and left Jenna wondering if she'd imagined the electricity that she'd felt arcing between them.

84

Ripping her gaze away, she tossed her purse and tote bag onto the passenger seat and climbed the rest of the way in as he used the remote to unlock his pickup truck, before turning back to her. "Look, I know you said you couldn't accept anything while Chris was still your student, but maybe when summer recess starts, Chris and I can take you out to dinner or something. It wouldn't be deemed inappropriate when he's no longer your student, right?"

If he hadn't thrown his nephew's name in there, Jenna might have thought he was asking her out on a date. But he had, so it would probably just be his way of thanking her for helping Chris pass. "Um . . . right. I guess it would be okay."

Holy hell, there were those adorable dimples that only appeared when a full smile graced his face. "Great. I'm looking forward to it. We'll revisit this conversation after finals' week. Drive safely, Jenna."

Without waiting for a response, he shut the door. When she just stared at him, he made a hand motion that she should hit the ignition button. Once her engine was running, he waved goodbye, spun around, and headed for his truck. Jenna couldn't tear her gaze away from his fine ass encased in the snug jeans. When he skirted around the front bumper and his lower half disappeared behind the vehicle, Jenna shook her head to clear it before putting her car in drive and pulling out of the space. It wasn't until she slowed while approaching the stop sign at the exit of the parking lot that she realized her thighs were tightly squeezed together. Damn. Summer recess couldn't come fast enough now.

CHAPTER SIX

hile Chris fiddled with the radio stations in the truck, Cade steered toward their favorite pizza place after a quick stop for gas. He hadn't intended to ask Jenna out today—he'd managed to stop himself from doing it in her classroom before offering to walk her to her car—but the words had come out of his mouth on their own accord. Thankfully, he'd added Chris to the scenario of them going out. That would change, though, after the kid was no longer her student. His attraction to her had been steadily growing each time he saw her, and he hoped it wasn't one sided. Summer recess couldn't come fast enough for him now.

Pulling into the parking lot of Manny's Pizzeria, Cade quickly found a space and the two hopped out of the truck. Holding the door open, he let his nephew walk into the half-filled restaurant first then followed. The two ate there every other Wednesday when Cade was off, and his mom went to Bingo Night at their church. The restaurant had been voted the best pizza in the county the past three years in a row. Every other pizzeria in the area paled in comparison in Cade's opinion.

"Hey, look. It's Ms. Anderson."

Cade followed his nephew's pointed finger, and sure enough, Jenna was standing in the line at the takeout counter. She turned when she heard her name and smiled at them. Striding toward her, Cade chuckled. "Are you following us?"

Her smile became wider at his teasing. "Um. I was here first, so I think I should be asking if *you're* following *me*. I didn't feel like cooking tonight, and it's been a while since I've treated myself to some of Manny's pizza. It's my favorite."

"Ours too. Listen, we're going to eat here; why don't you join us instead of getting takeout?" When she hesitated, he pressed on, not wanting the opportunity to get to know her better slip by. "Since it's just a coincidence we met here, it's not inappropriate for me to invite my nephew's teacher to join us to discuss how he's doing in class, right?"

Jenna glanced around at the other patrons. No one seemed to pay her and Cade any mind. "Um . . . right. I guess there's nothing wrong with having a guardian/teacher conference after we just happened to run into each other."

"Great." He scanned the seating area of the restaurant. "Booth or table?"

"Either. It doesn't matter to me," she responded at the same time Chris piped up.

"Booth."

Cade ruffled his nephew's hair. "I knew what your choice was, but it's always polite to ask the lady what she prefers." He gestured for Jenna to lead the way to an empty booth.

After they'd given their order of sodas and a pepperoni pizza to the college-aged man waiting on some of the tables, Chris, as usual, asked for money for the few video games that stood on the other side of the room. "Can I have two dollars this time, please? I got all my questions right."

"That you did." Cade pulled out his wallet. He usually only

allowed Chris to have $1.00 for the twenty-five-cent games, but Cade wanted more adult time with Jenna, so he easily caved. Handing over two one-dollar bills, he said, "Ask Lisa to tell you when our pizza is ready."

"Thanks! I will." Chris hurried toward his favorite video game without a backward glance, pausing only a moment to speak to the blonde waitress cleaning off a table.

Not wanting Jenna to think he knew the pretty woman intimately, he told her, "Lisa and my sister-in-law, Irene, were good friends."

"Oh. She's Manny's wife, right?"

"Yup." He was glad she knew that.

Usually on first dates, there were those awkward few moments before the two parties found a subject that enabled the conversation to flow freely. This time, however, Cade didn't experience that—not that they were on a date. Not really, although he wished they were. As she'd been since their first meeting over Chris's grades, Jenna was easy to talk to. She was smart, and unlike some women he'd dated, managed to hold a conversation that wasn't filled with words centered completely around her. She asked him questions about his job, training, and hobbies, and seemed genuinely interested in hearing his answers. In return, she'd answered his questions, as he struggled to keep them from being too personal. He was trying to not cross that line of guardian/teacher until Chris was no longer her student.

When their pizza was delivered to the table, Chris rejoined them, and the conversation turned to subjects to include him. The Fallon men were surprised to find out Jenna had been a Philadelphia Phillies fan since she'd been Chris's age and could rattle off players and statistics as easily as some sportscasters. The more she talked, the more Cade's attraction to her grew. And it was obvious Chris was smitten with his teacher. Jenna had chosen the best career for her personality. Cade was certain she'd be remembered fondly by her students for years to come.

"Oh my God! You're Mr. October, aren't you? Can we get a photo with you?"

Without waiting for an answer from a startled Cade, a couple of college-aged women whipped out a cellphone, leaned down next to him, and clicked off a few selfies, completely ignoring Jenna and Chris and the fact that Cade wasn't smiling. The blonde one then straightened and gave him a flirtatious smile. "What's your Instagram name? I'll tag you."

"I . . . um . . . don't have one." He did, but that was the one sage piece of advice he'd listened to from one of the guys who'd been in the first fire department calendar three years ago—don't give out your social media accounts to any of the women who approached him about it and keep the settings on private.

Blondie raised an eyebrow at him in disbelief. "Seriously?"

"Seriously," he responded, his irritation growing when he noticed Jenna's frown. "Now, if you'll excuse us, we're in the middle of dinner." Actually, Chris was the only one still eating, but his and Jenna's plates were still in front of them.

The grins across both the interlopers' faces dimmed a little as they finally noticed he wasn't alone. "Oh. Sorry." Blondie's disdain was clear as she shrugged before turning and walking away, her friend following.

Cade winced at Jenna. "I'm sorry about that."

"It happens all the time," Chris chimed in, much to his uncle's dismay. He didn't want Jenna to think he was a manwhore.

Unfortunately, he was certain that was her impression of him as she stood and pulled her wallet from her purse. "That's okay. I have to be going anyway. My dog is probably wondering why he doesn't have his own dinner yet."

Holding up a hand, Cade got to his feet. "Put away your money; dinner is on Chris and me tonight." When her smile returned, he knew it'd been a good idea to include Chris in that sentence.

"Thank you. And thank you for inviting me to join you."

"It was our pleasure." More than she'd probably ever know. *Two more weeks.* Two more weeks and he'd be able to ask her out on a real date, sans their petite chaperone.

"I'll see you tomorrow, Chris."

"Okay, Ms. Anderson. Can I give my book report first?" Reading was one of the boy's favorite subjects, probably because his mother had read to him almost every night of his life until her death.

Jenna smiled at his eagerness. "I'll put you at the top of the list."

"Let me walk you out," Cade said when she turned back to him with "goodbye" in her eyes.

"Thanks, but you don't have to."

"Actually, I want to." The blush he'd expected and received when he put the seductive lilt in his words stirred his desire once more. He might not be able to ask her out just yet, but the least he could do was let her know he was interested.

Glancing around quickly, Cade spotted Lisa and waved to her. "Can you watch Chris for a moment? I'll be right back."

Her hands full, the waitress gave him a nod. With a sweep of his hand, Cade gestured for Jenna to proceed him to the exit. When they reached the door, he reached around her and pushed it open, holding it for her.

"Thanks." Again, that blush appeared across her cheeks, and he wondered when the last time a man had treated her like she deserved to be treated—with utmost respect.

Now that they had more room than inside the restaurant, Cade walked beside her to her car. When they reached it and she unlocked the door, he once again opened it for her and waited for her to climb in. A whole bunch of cheesy phrases passed through his mind, but Jenna deserved better than a pickup line. *Two more weeks.* "Drive safely. I'll see you Friday afternoon."

She started the engine. "Great."

Unable to think of anything else to say to keep her there—she did say her dog was waiting for her—Cade said "goodbye" as he reluctantly closed the door. He shoved his hands into the pockets of his jeans as he watched her drive away. *Two more weeks.*

CHAPTER SEVEN

Ten Days Later . . .

Jenna woke up from the most erotic dream she'd had in a long time to find her hands between her legs, perilously close to a climax. In her mind, it was Cade stroking her clit and fucking her with his fingers. His tongue lapped at her distended nipple sending bolts of electricity to her core. Squirming, Jenna moaned the man's name as if it were a prayer. She could hear his response as he told her he wanted everything she could give him. *Come for me, Jenna.*

The orgasm hit her hard, practically blinding her as wave after wave tumbled over her. "Oh, God! Yes!" Her legs shook with the impact, until the sensations coursing through her body began to ebb.

Gulping for air, she let her limbs go lax. When she opened her eyes, she wasn't surprised to see Dudley sitting next to the bed, staring at her curiously. Usually if she was going to get herself off, she shut him out of the bedroom because it felt odd doing it while he was watching. She wasn't sure if it was because he was a dog or a male, but either way, it was weird. "Hope you enjoyed the show, Dud, because you won't be getting another one for a long time."

The dog's tail thumped on the floor in response before he gave a hopeful woof.

Jenna laughed as she glanced at the bedside clock. *6:00 a.m.* "All right, all right. I'll feed you fifteen minutes early. Just don't get used to it. I need all the beauty sleep I can get. Especially if I'm going to see Cade this afternoon."

"Woof." Dudley danced around the room as Jenna tossed aside the bed covers and stood, ready to start the day.

Thirty minutes later, the dog had been fed and Jenna had finished drying her hair. Putting on some makeup, she wasn't sure why she was even bothering. It wasn't as if Cade would be interested in her. In fact, she wasn't sure she wanted him to be after seeing how those skinny, pretty bimbos practically threw themselves at him last week at the pizzeria and hearing how it happened all the time. Of course it did. He was single, nice, employed, and a hunk of drool-worthy proportions. But the sad fact was she did want him, but he'd been nothing but polite to her these past few weeks. There had been a few times she'd thought he was flirting with her, but then he seemed to back off. He probably flirted with women all the time and didn't want Jenna to get the impression he wanted her or anything.

After dressing and gathering her things, she wished Dudley a good day and headed for her car. Suddenly, she remembered she hadn't grabbed her mail last night and walked to the box at the end of the drive to retrieve it. Once she was settled in the driver's seat of the Altima, she took a moment to shuffle through the bills and junk mail. At the bottom of the pile was a yellow flyer without an envelope. Unfolding it and spotting the reminder, she groaned. She'd completely forgotten all about the weekend carnival. Tonight and tomorrow night was the fire department's other big fundraiser of the year for the widows and orphans of the fallen. She wished they'd organized it for next weekend after finals, but someone had obviously not taken that into account during the planning stages. Jenna and Caroline had promised to help their friend Rachael with the funnel cake booth tonight at the large field behind the American Legion hall. Jenna would have just enough time after tutoring Chris to run home, change, and get there before the carnival goers started showing up.

When she pulled into the school, Caroline was getting out of her own vehicle, and Jenna parked next to her. Her friend smiled as Jenna climbed out and shut the car door.

"My, don't you look nice today. Let me guess, Chris Fallon has his last tutoring session this afternoon, and Uncle Hottie is picking him up afterward."

Jenna rolled her eyes. "Yes, it's the last session before the final. And, no, I didn't dress up for Cade; I just felt like wearing this today."

"Mm-hm. If you say so." Her tone said she didn't believe a word Jenna had said.

Thankfully, her friend dropped the subject as they strode toward the front entrance to the school. This time of year was always bittersweet for Jenna. She was looking forward to her summer vacation, yet she didn't want to say goodbye to her students. Every year, she fell in love with her class—their eagerness to learn was still there in the third grade—and it saddened her knowing she wouldn't be teaching them ever again. But a new class would start in September, and the whole cycle would begin again. This year, it looked like every one of her students would be passing, including Chris. The one-on-one sessions had helped him tremendously and Jenna had no doubts about him doing well on the final.

Another thought hit her. This would probably be the last day she'd be seeing Cade. Wasn't that a huge bummer. She'd gotten used to seeing him three times a week, and having the uncle and nephew walk her to her car. They'd chat about all sorts of things, but not once had they invited her to join them for dinner again.

Nor had Cade mentioned anything again about wanting to take her out during summer recess to thank her for tutoring Chris. Although it was for the best, Jenna couldn't help but feel disappointment over it. Clearly, Cade had only invited her to eat with them that evening because it'd been the polite thing to do after running into her at the pizzeria. She obviously wasn't his type which was a party girl and not someone he could take home to his mother.

Striding into her classroom, Jenna flipped the light switch, then got settled in to start the day. She tried unsuccessfully to not count down the minutes before she'd see Cade again. *Damn it.*

"GET those hoses to the west side! Fallon! Morris! We've got a report of an elderly woman trapped on the second-floor bedroom at the end of the hall. Go get her, boys! Murray! Peterman! Get on the roof and ventilate that sucker!"

The chief continued to bark out orders as the rest of the firemen poured off the fire trucks and rushed to do their assigned tasks. The residential fire was in full bloom on the west side of the two-story home with flames shooting out several windows and climbing toward the roof. Gray smoke rolled out of every available crevice, tumbling into the air. From where they stood, threading their arms through the straps of their Scott Air-Packs, Cade and Jack Morris could feel the intense heat of the fire.

After their oxygen supplies were settled on their backs, the two men pulled the masks down over their faces and raced toward the front entrance of the home where two of their teammates had already rammed the door in. They had a hose aimed at the flames licking the ceiling of the living room to the right of the door. Cade and Jack Morris turned on their flashlights as they entered and took the stairs to the left up to the second floor, with Cade leading the way. Even through his protective gear, he felt like a turkey roasting in an oven. The smoke was so dense, he couldn't see more than a few inches in front of his face. Upon reaching the second-floor landing, he dropped to his knees to crawl under the layers of smoke. It gave him a little more sight distance but not much. Feeling his way down the corridor, he made sure the woman hadn't tried to escape the fire and collapsed along the way. Since the victim was reported to be at the bedroom at the end of the hall, they'd start there. If she wasn't found, they'd search the other two bedrooms and bathroom.

There were no cries for help. The only thing Cade could hear was the roar of the inferno behind them and the sounds of his and Morris's breathing through their masks. Finally, his hand hit the door at the end of the hallway. It was shut. Reaching up, he found the knob, turned it and pushed the door open. It was smoky in the room but not as bad as the rest of the house. Getting to his feet, Cade hurried over to the bed where the elderly woman lay prone. "Chief, this is Rescue 5. Missing located. Confirm no one else is in here."

"Confirmed, Rescue 5. Got a family member here now; says that should be the only one inside."

Not wasting time, Cade rolled the small, fragile woman onto her back and then picked her up into a fireman's carry over his shoulder. Turning, he placed one hand on Morris's shoulder. The other man would lead the way out, using the cable he'd let out behind them on the way in. It would help them get out much faster than crawling. As they made their way down the hall, they heard part of the roof collapse at the back of the house.

"Shit!" Morris spat. "Let's get the hell out of here!"

"You don't have to tell me twice, man; move it!"

They clambered down the stairs as quickly as they dared on the wet tile. Their teammates spotted them and pointed the high-pressured hose at the nearby flames, giving the two men and their victim room to pass out into the fresh air. Cade carried the woman to where several EMTs were waiting, before setting her down gently onto the grass. Ripping off his mask, he stepped back and gave them room to work. Relief coursed through him when one of them announced the victim had a pulse and was breathing. An oxygen mask was placed over her face while another EMT hooked her up to an EKG monitor.

A younger woman rushed up to Cade. "Thank you! Oh, my God! Thank you for saving my mother."

She threw her arms around him, ignoring the fact he was dirty and soaking wet, reeking of smoke. Cade patted her on the back. "I hope she's okay, ma'am. You'll be able to go to the hospital with her."

The woman nodded and backed away. Tears were rolling down her cheeks as she thanked him once again, then grabbed her mother's hand as she was transferred to a stretcher.

Shrugging off his Scott pack, Cade turned to Morris and grinned. "All in a day's work."

Morris chuckled and jutted his chin toward the woman climbing into the ambulance after her mother. "Better than one of your adoring fans hugging you, I bet."

"Damn straight." He glanced at the house and saw the rest of the squad was getting the fire under control. Unfortunately, the one side of the structure was pretty much a goner. It was a good thing he'd contacted his mom when the call came in twenty minutes before the end of the shift. He'd been looking forward to seeing Jenna again when he picked up Chris, but there was no way he was going to make it in time. They'd be here for at least another hour, putting out the hotspots and tearing down any walls that were in danger of falling. After that, it would take a while to pack up all the hoses and gear, then everything had to be cleaned back at the station. Used oxygen tanks would have to be refilled and equipment would have to be checked. Following a shower, he'd then have to go pick Chris up for the carnival.

Maybe he'd have his mother and Chris just meet him at the American Legion; it would save Cade from driving back and forth. The kid had been anticipating going to the carnival all week. Cade was scheduled to be at the dunking booth for a half hour and then at the calendar signing booth for another thirty minutes. His nephew was dying to send him into the tank of water and with the pitching arm he was developing, it wouldn't be a surprise if he did it.

Too bad Cade wasn't going to see Jenna this afternoon. He would have liked to invite her to the carnival, but maybe it was for the better. He had five more days to go before he could ask her out. With all the fantasies of her he'd been having these past few weeks, he just prayed she didn't turn him down.

CHAPTER EIGHT

"*T*he next time we agree to help out, make sure it's not a booth that has me sweating grease."

Jenna agreed with Caroline. It was hot as hell under the funnel cake tent, and the oil boiling behind them wasn't helping. They were both dying to take showers, but still had another half hour before their shifts were over and two other women replaced them. Jenna felt the grease in her pores. Thank God Rachael had brought a stash of baby wipes for everyone to clean up with.

After handing out two more plates of the fried dough covered in confectioner's sugar, Jenna swiped her brow with her forearm. The temperature had been climbing all day and was now holding steady at 78 degrees, and it was already 8:00 p.m. The carnival would be open for three more hours. She wondered where Cade was. There were a lot of firemen walking around and working in different booths, but she hadn't seen him. His mother had mentioned he'd be there when she'd picked up Chris because Cade had gotten a late call at work.

"Hi, Ms. Anderson!"

Speak of the devil—or at least two of them. "Hi, Chris. Hi, Mrs. Fallon. Enjoying the carnival?"

"Yup," the boy said with a grin. "It'll be even better when Uncle Cade finishes at the calendar booth and takes me on the rides. Grandma doesn't like the ones that make your stomach flip."

"I had enough stomach-flipping excitement when I was younger," Mrs. Fallon said with a grin. "I'll leave it up to you now."

"Can I get a funnel cake, Grandma?" The boy definitely had the puppy-dog look down pat—the one that was going to make every female want to hug him when he got older.

"Sure." She took money out of her wallet and handed it to Jenna. "We'll get your Uncle Cade one too. It's always been his favorite treat at carnivals." She winked at Jenna. "Cade's got an enormous sweet tooth—you know he's single, right?"

Jenna felt a faint blush stain her cheeks. It was obvious the older woman was trying to set her up with Cade. "Um . . . I think he mentioned that one day. Here's your change." She glanced at Chris. "With sugar?"

His eyes lit up. "Yes, please! Lots of it!"

Before Jenna turned to get two plates of funnel cake, she noticed Mrs. Fallon give her a hand signal that told her to take it easy on the sweet, white powder. She didn't want to be the reason her student was bouncing off the walls tonight because he was on a sugar overload. When she handed over the plates to Chris, he seemed to be satisfied with them. "Thanks, Ms. Anderson. Here, Grandma, hold mine. I'll run and give Uncle Cade his."

The boy took off, and Jenna's gaze followed him all the way to the red tent on the other side of the field. She caught glimpses of Cade through the crowd milling about. He was sitting behind a table with two other firemen from the calendar, and there was a long line of women of all ages waiting for autographs from the trio. Many of the women were doing their best to show off their figures in tight shorts or skirts and skimpy tops with plunging necklines.

Handing a signed calendar back to a woman, Cade's face brightened when his nephew approached. Taking the sweet treat from Chris, his gaze followed where the boy was pointing back to the funnel tent. His smile grew wider when he spotted Jenna. At least she thought it did—it could be because he saw his mother. Cade turned and said something to one of the firemen standing behind him. The other man nodded then took Cade's place when he stood. Jenna could see several disappointed women staring after him as he strode across the field, his gaze pinned to Jenna. Yup, she could now say for sure he was looking at her and not his mother—unless he had an Oedipus complex which she doubted. There was desire in his eyes, and it stunned her. She couldn't take her eyes off him—it was as if the crowd had disappeared and only the two of them existed.

"Don't forget, dear, he's single and quite the catch. And I'm not just saying that because he's my son. If I'm not mistaken, he's just as interested in you as you are in him."

Startled by Mrs. Fallon's words and observation, Jenna's blush bloomed as the woman winked at her, waved to her son, then walked over to join several people her own age. Realizing she'd been caught staring at the hunky fireman, Jenna quickly spun around and tried to busy herself, but unfortunately there were no new customers. In fact, her relief had arrived and told her she would take over. Caroline handed Jenna a few baby wipes they'd been using to battle the grease and sweat, and with a compelling look, silently ordered her to turn around and face Cade.

"Hi, Jenna."

She couldn't ignore Cade, nor did she want to. She quickly wiped her face, neck, and arms, then tossed the wipes into the garbage. Taking a deep breath, she steadied herself to face him again. When she did a one-eighty, though, the wicked look she'd seen in his eyes moments earlier was gone. In its place was a friendly one—had she misread things moments ago? "Hi, Cade." She gestured toward the calendar tent. "Having fun?"

Frowning, he glanced over his shoulder before his smile returned when he looked at her again. "Not really, but I'm looking forward to some now. I'm done at the signing, and it sounds like you're done here too, so why don't you join Chris and I on a few rides."

"Um . . . I . . . I was going to walk around with Caroline for a bit."

Her friend jumped forward. "Actually, I'm kind of tired." She dramatically wiped her brow. "*Phew*. Long day. I think I'll just go home, take a nice bath, and read for a while. You kids run along and have some fun."

As Cade chuckled at Caroline, Jenna rolled her eyes at her friend. "Yeah, that was subtle."

"I never claimed to be subtle." She gently pushed Jenna toward the end of the table separating them from their customers. "Go on. Have some fun."

"C'mon, Ms. Anderson! We'll go on the Spider first!" Chris was bouncing on his feet in anticipation.

Cade's hand reached toward her, but then he seemed to think better of it and dropped it. "Hope you like rides that spin around like crazy. Those are his favorite."

"I love them, actually," she responded as they walked side by side in the direction of the ride Chris was hurrying toward. "I was the daredevil in my family. Put my brothers to shame all the time."

Grinning, Cade raised an eyebrow at her. "The wild child, huh? How many brothers do you have?"

"Three. I'm the youngest and the only girl." She already knew it had just been Cade and his brother Caleb, so she didn't inquire about other siblings. Instead, she asked, "So, did you always want to be a fireman growing up?"

"Hell, yeah. I dressed up as a fireman practically every Halloween. As soon as I graduated college, I took the test. I'd wanted to take it sooner, but a friend of my dad's was on the fire department and convinced me that if I wanted to climb the ranks one day, the degree would help."

"Do you want to do that? I mean, climb the ranks one day?"

They got on the end of a line with Chris, waiting for the Spider ride to stop and let the current occupants off. "Definitely. In fact, I've already started studying for the promotion exam that's coming up in October."

She had no doubt he'd do well on the test. "Good luck. I'll keep my fingers crossed for you."

"Thanks."

The huskiness in his voice had her gaze meeting his, and there was that heat again. This time, there was no mistaking it. Jenna was at a loss for words. She thanked the powers that be that she had on a bra with some padding to it because she could feel her nipples become taut. Her panties were damp as desire spiraled through her. She was far from a virgin, and had dated several men over the years, but none of them had looked at her like Cade was doing now. None of them had made her feel like she was the only woman in the world. *Holy hell.*

"C'mon, Uncle Cade! It's our turn." Chris's excited voice broke the spell between them, and Jenna ducked her head and tucked several strands of hair behind her ear.

There was enough room in the ride's car for the three of them, and Chris sat between them. They laughed as the Spider's arms rotated, then sloped up and down. After they finished on that ride, they went to all the others, then redid their favorites. Jenna couldn't remember the last time she'd had so much fun. The only time her stomach clenched was when she caught several women during the evening giving her dirty looks and Cade seductive ones. But the man seemed oblivious to all of them. If one of them interrupted the threesome's conversations, he politely disengaged from them. Although, he did take a few moments to sign some more calendars. But if Jenna stepped toward the side to give him and his adoring fans room, he closed the distance again and winked at her.

Damn, the man was good for her ego.

CHAPTER NINE

*B*y the time Chris's energy was finally winding down and yawning, Jenna couldn't shake the feeling that she and Cade had been on a date, albeit a chaperoned one. Disappointment that the night was ending rolled through her as he escorted her to her car. Mrs. Fallon had rejoined them a short time ago and told Cade she'd drive Chris home in her car—because of his late call with the fire department, they'd arrived in separate vehicles.

Jenna unlocked her Altima, then faced Cade. "Thanks for the great time tonight. I enjoyed myself. I forgot how much fun it was to go on all the rides."

"I had fun too," Cade responded as he opened the door for her. "Maybe we can do it again sometime? I'd like to take you out on a date."

Her eyes widened. "A date?"

His brow shot up. "You do date, don't you? Or are you in a relationship with someone?"

"N-No. I mean, I do date. I'm just not dating anyone right now." She was off-kilter, uncertain of his intentions. "Are you sure?"

It was his turn to be confused. "Am I sure, what?"

"Um . . . are you sure you're asking me out on a date?"

His brow furrowed. "Am I sure? Um, yeah. I don't think I would've asked if I hadn't been sure." Cade chuckled and scratched his temple. "We're kinda stumbling over this whole thing, aren't we?" When Jenna silently nodded, he continued. "Okay. Let's try this again a little more clearly. I'm attracted to you, Jenna. I'd like to get to know you better. I know you can't date a student's parent or guardian, so I'll have to wait until school is over and Chris is no longer in your class. Then, I'd like to take you out to dinner one night—just the two of us." He frowned slightly. "That is, unless you're not attracted to me."

"I am!" Her face heated in embarrassment. Jenna couldn't remember the last time she'd been so flustered by a man. Then again, her last real date had been over a year ago. It wasn't that she hadn't been asked, but she'd always felt that if there wasn't some sort of immediate allure between two people, the date would be a disaster. As a result, she'd turned a few requests down over the past fourteen or fifteen months. Thank goodness that wasn't the case this time—she was definitely interested in him. "I mean, I—I am attracted to you. But you're right. We'd have to wait for summer recess to . . . um . . . go out . . . on a date."

Jenna's gaze roamed his handsome face. He had gorgeous eyelashes that fanned his cheeks when he blinked. His eyes danced as he studied her, patiently waiting for an answer. His lips were perfection, just like the rest of him, and she wondered what they'd feel like against hers. Was he a skillful lover? She was almost certain he was. What she wouldn't give to be one hundred percent sure.

The corners of his mouth ticked upward. "Glad we got that settled. Now, I think you'd better get in your car and drive home. It's taking everything inside of me not to pull you into my arms and kiss the hell out of you." Jenna's eyes widened, and that made Cade chuckle. "Oh, yes, Ms. Anderson—I'm hot for the teacher.

More than you probably realize, but I'm hanging on by a thread until school is out next week." He took her elbow and urged her into the driver's seat. "Just be advised, though, that after the last bell on Wednesday, I plan on kissing you the first chance I get. Now, please get your sweet ass in the car so I can go home and take a cold shower."

Jenna couldn't help it. Now that she was sitting in the car, a certain part of his anatomy was right in front of her, and her eyes zoomed in on it. The bulge there couldn't be missed. Her pussy throbbed, and her mouth watered at the thought of what was behind the denim jeans he wore.

When Cade cleared his throat, she knew she'd been caught staring. Her entire body flushed in embarrassment, and she dropped her gaze to the ground. His deep voice had her heart rate spiking when he said, "Look at me, Jenna." When she did, he smiled. There was no cockiness or teasing in his expression, just a combination of want and need that he seemed to be trying to control. "Drive safe. I'll see you Wednesday."

All she could do was nod and swing her legs into the car before he closed her door. Her hands shook as she started the engine and put the car in drive. Swallowing hard, she gave Cade a wave then drove away.

CADE CHECKED the clock on his dashboard for the third time in five minutes. Two more and the school bell would ring, signaling the end of the school year and the start of his seduction of one Jenna Anderson. The last few days since the carnival had been torture. His daily showers had included jack-off sessions while imagining her on her knees before him and those plump lips of hers around his cock. And damn, that had him getting hard again. He ran the starting lineup of the Philadelphia Phillies through his mind, not wanting a prominent hard-on when hundreds of kids filled the parking lot.

The clock changed to 2:50 p.m., and Cade could hear the school bell go off through the open classroom windows. Climbing out of the car, he strode to the front of it and leaned against the grill. He crossed his arms and ankles, then waited. A tidal wave of kids came rushing out of the school, most heading toward the line of yellow buses. A few ran to where a crossing guard stood sentry, waiting to walk them across the street to the housing development on the other side. Still, others found their parents' cars in the parking lot.

Cade had told Chris he'd pick him up today instead of letting the boy take the bus home. His reasoning had been two-fold. They were going to the Game Stop store for Chris to pick out a new game to celebrate passing all his classes. He'd done well enough on the last two math exams and the final to finish the year with a C average. It wasn't the greatest, but it was far better than failing. The rest of his grades had been all Bs and As. The second reason for picking Chris up was so Cade could see Jenna and make plans for their date. If he had his wish, they'd be going out to dinner tonight. Cade's mom had been more than happy to watch Chris for him. She'd made it known that she approved of him dating Jenna. He was sure that if they were still together by the end of the summer, his mother would be planning their wedding, with or without their input. For the first time in his life, that thought didn't scare the hell out of him. Jenna was special, and he intended on proving it to her.

Chris came running over to him and jumped up and down. "Uncle Cade, can I go to Tommy Berger's house?" He pointed to where his friend was walking with his mother toward a minivan. "His mom invited me over for a barbecue to celebrate the end of school. Can I go?"

Smiling, Cade kept one eye on his nephew and the other on the front door to the school. He didn't want to miss Jenna coming out, although he was sure he had time. "It's 'may I,' and I thought you wanted to go to Game Stop."

"I do, but I want to go to Tommy's too. Please! Can—I mean, may I?" His hands were clasped together as he begged.

Cade pushed off the car. "Sure, kiddo. Let me go talk to Mrs. Berger and get the details. We'll go shopping tomorrow."

"Yay!"

Chris ran ahead as Cade followed. A few minutes later, Chris was climbing into the minivan and waving goodbye to his uncle. Tracy Berger had extended the invitation, and Chris would be sleeping over at her house tonight, much to the two boys' delight. Cade would drop off some clothes for his nephew later.

It wasn't long before the buses pulled away and the parking lot emptied out. Cade knew Jenna hadn't come out yet because her car was still there. He went back to his original position, resting against the front of his truck. Finally, the door opened, and Jenna strolled out with Caroline. The blonde was the first to notice him and elbowed her friend. Grinning, Caroline waved at him, then headed for her own car as Jenna slowly approached him.

"Hi," she greeted him, stopping a few feet away. Her apprehension at his presence was evident and turning him on. She wasn't scared of him, just unsure of where they stood with each other. Something he planned on rectifying.

"Hi, yourself. Happy summer recess."

He swallowed a groan when her tongue peeked out to wet her lips. "Thanks." She glanced into his truck. "Where's Chris?"

"He went home with Tracy Berger and Tommy for a barbecue and sleepover." Pushing off the truck, he closed the distance between them and reached up. He ran his fingers through a few strands of her hair, confirming they were as soft as they looked. Her eyes widened but she didn't move away. Cade glanced at his watch. "It's 3:05—you're no longer Chris's teacher. Will you go out with me tonight to dinner and put me out of my misery?"

The corners of her luscious mouth pulled up into a smile that had his heart beating faster. "And why are you in misery?"

"Because I've been lusting after my nephew's teacher since the moment I laid eyes on her and I can't get her out of my mind. Because I want to get to know her better than I already do, especially what it's like to kiss her."

When the pupils in her eyes flared and her mouth dropped open at his last words, Cade couldn't stop himself. He leaned down and found out what he'd been dying to know. *Heaven.* She tasted like heaven as he brushed his lips across hers. As he was about to deepen the kiss, the front door of the school opening sounded louder than normal in the silence of the nearly-empty parking lot, and Jenna jumped back, her eyes filled with desire, and her cheeks tinged with pink. One of the other teachers strode out, completely unaware of what he'd just interrupted.

Cade cleared his throat. Making out with his nephew's teacher—former teacher—in the parking lot, fifteen minutes after the end of the school year, was probably not a good idea. After the other man got in his car and drove away, Cade shoved his hands in his pockets to keep from reaching for Jenna again. "Rest assured I want to kiss you again—and for much longer— but I'd like to buy you dinner first. May I?"

Appearing breathless, Jenna nodded. "I'd like that."

He wasn't sure which part she was referring to—the kiss or dinner—but either way, he knew he was going to enjoy it.

CHAPTER TEN

Sitting in the passenger seat of Cade's truck, Jenna forced herself to relax. Dinner had been wonderful, but the entire time she'd been anticipating what would happen afterward. That all-too-brief kiss they'd shared in the school parking lot was still fresh in her mind. She'd heard people say that fireworks went off when you finally met the one person who'd been made for you, but she had always thought it was a metaphor. Boy, had she been wrong. In those mere seconds that their lips had been touching, her world had exploded. If it hadn't been for Scott Grayson coming out of the school at that exact moment, Jenna was sure she and Cade would have been pulled into a full-blown make-out session.

After giving her two hours to go home, take care of Dudley, then get ready for their date, Cade had picked her up at her house. She usually didn't let a guy do that on the first date, but she felt as if the last two months of seeing Cade a few times a week had been a form of . . . well, foreplay. They'd talked a lot that night they'd met at the pizzeria, and more at the carnival, but there had been plenty of shorter conversations when he'd walked her to her car each time he picked Chris up after the tutoring sessions. She had no idea if Cade planned on kissing her again on her doorstep, but the heated looks he'd been giving her during dinner had her thinking he would. She hoped like hell he did, because she was dying to find out if those fireworks from earlier had been a fluke.

She glanced over at him. Damn, he was gorgeous. He'd shaven for their date and his jaw appeared baby soft. His dark hair also looked like he'd gotten a trim since that afternoon. The white, button-down shirt he wore fit his torso like a glove before disappearing into his black trousers. The man was sin on two long legs.

Her mouth went dry as he turned down her street and pulled into her driveway. As he'd done at the restaurant, he told her to wait while he came around and opened her door. After helping her down, he shut the door and escorted her up the walkway to her front steps. Before she could retrieve her keys to open the door that Dudley was barking behind, Cade took her hand and turned her to face him. Desire filled his eyes, and she felt her own body responding to it. Without a word, he leaned down, and his mouth took possession of hers. All thought fled Jenna's mind. She couldn't think at all, only feel. His lips were both hard and soft, urging her to open her own and let him in, as he pulled her flush against his chest. She didn't hesitate.

Jenna had no idea where this attraction between them was going, but she knew she wanted to find out. Never had being in a man's arms felt so right. Not once during their date, or any of the other times they'd been together, had his gaze roamed to the other women around them. He'd always been focused on her. He'd pulled out her chair for her, opened doors, put himself between her and the street on sidewalks, and did other things to make her feel special.

His hands clutched her hips, and his erection was prominent. His tongue dueled with hers, searching, tasting every inch of her mouth. Without warning he ended the kiss. Breathless, he touched his forehead to hers. "You have no idea how much I want you to ask me to stay, but I don't want to rush you. I want you, Jenna. More than any woman I've ever met. If you tell me to leave, I will, but rest assured, I'll be taking you out on another date as soon as I can. And again and again, because I don't ever think I'll be able to get enough of you. I don't want to scare you, but I'm falling for you, baby. I've been falling in love with you since the moment I met you. Just kissing you was worth the wait. Please, let me come in for a little while. Even if we don't go any further tonight than this, I'm just not ready to let you out of my arms yet. We can just sit and cuddle and talk if that's what you want."

There was no way she was sending him away. Not with the way he'd made her body sing in the past few minutes. Not after that speech he just gave. Taking a step back, she quickly located her keys in the outside pocket of her purse, then handed them to him with the one for the house separated from the others. Heat flared in his eyes when he realized she was letting him stay. He opened the door, and Jenna introduced him to Dudley who took all of three seconds to decide this new human could enter his domain.

After making sure the dog was set for the night with his water and treats, Jenna turned to Cade, suddenly nervous again. "Um . . . can I get you something to drink?"

He shook his head as he took her hand and pulled her close again. "The only thing I want right now is you."

Cade kissed her again as if the last few minutes hadn't happened. Almost on their own volition, her palms flattened on his hard chest, then dragged upward to wrap around his neck and into his hair. His mouth devoured hers as his hands dropped to her ass and cupped the two orbs. He ground his pelvis into hers and Jenna knew right then and there they'd be in her bed soon. She wanted this man, more than she wanted her next breath. This time, it was her turn to halt the kiss.

"Are you okay?" he asked. His lips were wet and swollen, and his hair was mussed from her fingers. "Too fast?"

She took his hand and tugged him toward her bedroom. "Not at all." A thought crossed her mind. Jenna stopped and turned toward him. "Please don't think I do this all the time. It's been a long time since I've had a man in my house and in my bed. This doesn't seem rushed to me. I feel like we've been leading up to this for the past two months. I have no doubts, and I won't have any regrets."

"Neither will I, but if you want to stop, just say the word, and I'll abide by it." His words were the truth; she could see it in his eyes. Cade wasn't the only one who'd been falling since they'd first met.

Jenna led him to her bedroom, glad she'd taken the time to straighten up after trying on ten different outfits earlier. She was thankful she'd gone with the little black dress and heels, since she'd caught Cade staring at her legs several times during the evening.

Cade closed the door behind them, keeping Dudley out. They didn't need a canine audience. Before Jenna could turn around to face him, Cade's hands grasped her shoulders, holding her in place. He whispered in her ear, sending shivers down her spine. "I've been undressing you all night in my head. Let me do it now for real."

"Yes." Jenna didn't recognize the throaty response as coming from her mouth. All she wanted was to feel Cade's hands on her naked skin and to touch him in return.

With a slow and painstaking motion, he lowered the zipper of the dress at her back. After peeling the sleeves off her arms, he pushed the material down her body. His lips trailed down her spine, all the way to the indent above her panty-covered ass. The dress pooled at her feet. Cade's hands went to her hips, turning her in place as he kissed his way around to her abdomen. Jenna tensed, and he froze. His worried gaze found her face. "What's wrong?"

Embarrassed, she tilted her head back and stared at the ceiling. "Sorry, I'm not used to a man kissing me all over like that. If you hadn't noticed, I'm not exactly skinny."

Cade jumped to his feet, startling her. His face had hardened. Grabbing her shoulders, he spun her around again until she was facing the oval, full length mirror on the outside of her bathroom door. He cupped her chin and lifted it up. "Look at yourself." His eyes met hers in the reflection as he kissed the bra strap on her shoulder. "I don't know what you think I like in a woman, Jenna, but it's not skinny. Most men like curves on their women." He ran his hands up and down her sides, heating up said curves. His mouth nuzzled her neck as he cupped her breasts, feeling their weight. "You're beautiful, baby. Absolutely stunning. I was telling you the truth before. I've wanted you since the moment I turned around and you said you were Chris's teacher. I got hard as a rock watching your ass as you walked back into the school. Trust me—I love your body and plan on kissing every inch of it."

Pulling down the cups of her bra, he left it below her breasts, pushing them upward. His fingers plucked her peaked nipples, his gaze pinned on their reflection in the mirror. He pressed his hard cock against her ass, and Jenna groaned.

"Like that, baby? That's all for you. You did that to me. You do that to me every time you walk into a room. I have no doubts you'll be doing that to me fifty years from now." Cade slid a hand down her abdomen and cupped her sex. "Shit, baby, you're hot and wet for me. You're going to burn me alive—good thing I'm a fireman. I'll stoke the flames inside you, then make you come for me over and over again." His fingers pushed aside the small scrap of satin separating him from her core. He parted her labia and curled his fingers inward.

Jenna's hips bucked forward as one then two fingers entered her. "Oh, God!"

Cade growled and removed his hand. Before she knew what he was doing, he'd ripped her panties from her body. "I'll buy you new ones." His fingers returned to where they'd been torturing her, the heel of his hand grinding against her clit. "I want you to come for me, baby. I want to see you shatter for me. Put your arms up around my neck and hold on."

She did as she was told, losing herself in the arousal coursing through her body. Never had any of her lovers taken her from zero to sixty in such a short time. Cade played her like a fine Stradivarius. He stroked her, licked her, kissed her, taking her higher and higher. Jenna's legs trembled as she reached for her climax. His fingers plunged in and out of her core, faster, harder. His mouth went to the shell of her ear. "Come for me, baby."

When he nipped her lobe, Jenna screamed as the orgasm hit her like a thunderbolt. The room filled with fireworks as her body shook. She would have collapsed onto the floor if Cade hadn't been holding her up. The tremors seemed to go on for hours, but in reality, it was far less. Finally, she sagged against him. "Holy shit!"

He chuckled against her neck. "That's just for starters, baby."

Bending down, Cade swooped her up into his arms like she weighed no more than a feather, before depositing her on the bed. She popped back up and reached for the belt around his waist. While she worked on that, Cade found the clasp of her bra and released her from its confines. When she undid the zipper of his pants, they fell to the floor. He unbuttoned his shirt in record time, then added it to the growing pile of clothes. Jenna licked her lips as she stared at the cotton covered hard-on before her.

Cade groaned. "Damn, baby. If you keep staring at it like that it's gonna explode before I ever get inside you."

A giggle escaped her. "Sorry, but it's quite impressive, and I haven't even seen it in the flesh yet."

"Well, let me accommodate you." He shoved his boxer briefs to the floor, then stood there in all his glory. Impressive had been an understatement. His cock was gorgeous, just like the rest of Cade. Reaching out, Jenna wrapped her hand around it, and Cade let out a muttered curse as his hips thrust forward. A bead of pre-cum eased from the slit at the tip of the dark tip. He felt like velvet against her palm and fingers as she stroked him. Cade's head fell back on his shoulders as his eyes slammed shut. He let her indulge for a few moments before stepping back. "It'll be over way too soon if I let you keep doing that."

Glancing down, he located his pants, then retrieved his wallet. After taking out a condom, he tossed the wallet onto her night stand. She watched as he sheathed himself, and her body began to hum in anticipation. Cade crawled onto the bed and over her, settling his hips between her legs. His mouth found hers again. The coarse hairs on his chest rasped across her nipples, which made her pussy weep. Supporting himself on his forearms, Cade tilted his hips. Jenna felt the tip of his cock at her entrance and spread her legs wider for him. He eased inside her as her body yielded to him. She moaned as he rocked his hips back and forth, gaining ground with each stroke until he was completely inside her warmth.

Jenna could feel how he was restraining himself, and she didn't want him to. She wanted all of him. She wanted him to love her hard and fast until they both screamed their combined releases. Bringing her legs up, she wrapped them around his hips and dug her heels into his taut ass. "Make me come again, Cade. Make us both come."

He withdrew almost all the way out of her channel before thrusting back in. His hips moved faster and faster. "Damn, baby. You feel so damn good. So tight. So hot. You're on fire down there."

Her body was climbing again, as Cade worshiped it with his hands, mouth, and cock. Her walls began to quiver around him. "That's it, baby. You're like a vise. Come for me."

Without slowing his pace, Cade reached between them and

found her clit with his thumb. When he pressed down, Jenna flew, taking him with her. They both shouted as their bodies found the ultimate bliss. Gasping for air, Cade collapsed on top of her, but she didn't mind his weight at all. They lay there, basking in the afterglow for several minutes before Cade lifted his head. He brushed his lips across hers. "Baby, you just rocked my world, and I can't wait for you to do it again."

Neither could she.

EPILOGUE

One Year Later . . .

*W*alking up and down the aisles between the desks in her classroom, Jenna handed her students back their final math exams as they chattered excitedly about their summer plans. Everyone had passed the third grade with flying colors, and tomorrow would be the last day of school. As it had been last year and every other year since she'd become a teacher, this final week was bittersweet. She'd miss this class as much as she missed all the ones that had come before it. But she did have something to look forward to this year.

This time next week, she'd be in Disney World with Cade and Chris. They'd also be meeting two of Jenna's brothers and their wives and children there. Somehow, a routine conversation about her summer plans had resulted in a mini family reunion in Florida. After Cade, Chris, Mrs. Fallon, and Caroline had gone to Jenna's hometown with her at Christmas, her parents and brothers had approved of her relationship with the hunky fireman. It had been a wonderful holiday with everyone she loved.

After telling the children to take their seats, Jenna turned on the movie that appeared on the white board at the front of the classroom. She'd promised them if they all passed, which she already knew they would, she'd let them watch Disney's version of Pocahontas. With the finals over, there wasn't much else she needed to take care of.

About ten minutes into the movie, the fire alarm resounded through the building. The teachers had been notified about the morning drill, but they hadn't known what time. Apparently, the fire inspector wanted to observe the drill to make sure everything was done properly. Jenna quickly shut off the movie and told the children to line up at the door. As they'd practiced numerous times throughout the year, they exited the classroom, single file, and proceeded out to the playground, far away from the building. It wasn't long before they heard the sirens of the fire engines approaching, and Jenna realized she would probably see Cade. He was working today and his station was the closest. She didn't get to see him often in his full gear, but she stopped by the station about once a week to just say hi and bring him and his squad freshly-made cookies that didn't come from a bakery.

Caroline stepped over to her and rolled her eyes. "They had to do this two days before the end of school? Seriously?"

"Better than in the middle of exams," she responded, her gaze searching the men, dressed in their turnout gear, climbing off the engine and ladder truck that had pulled into the circular drive in front of the school. She spotted Cade and was surprised to see him jogging across the grass to where she stood with her students. His eyes were pinned on her, and she was so wrapped up in the heat she saw there, she didn't realize that none of the firemen were going inside the school. They were standing by the trucks, watching the activity on the field.

Cade grinned as he stopped in front of her. "Hi. You know, I was wracking my brain on how to do this right, and thought why not do it where we first met."

Her brow narrowed in confusion. The students and teachers around her had gone quiet but it didn't register in her mind. "What are you talking about?"

To her shock, Cade got down on one knee. Her eyes went wide, and her mouth dropped open as he held out a small jeweler's box with the most stunning diamond ring she'd ever seen. Chris stood just behind Cade, his eyes filled with glee as his uncle took Jenna's hand. "Ms. Jenna Anderson, you are the light of my life. I never thought I'd meet a woman who would complete me, but I did. And that woman is you. You're everything I never knew was missing in my life. I love you, baby. Will you marry me and become Mrs. Jenna Fallon?"

"And my aunt!" Chris shouted.

Cade chuckled. "That too. We're sort of a package deal."

Tears were rolling down Jenna's cheeks, and she couldn't stop them to save her life. She nodded several times before she finally found her voice, but it only came out as a hoarse whisper. "Y-Yes. Yes, I'll marry you. Yes, I'll be Chris's aunt. Yes, I love you."

Taking the ring from the box, he slid it on the correct finger of her left hand. Getting to his feet, he glanced over his shoulder. "She said yes!"

His squad whooped it up, as did the students and teachers. Someone on the fire engine pulled the airhorn cord several times in celebration as Cade picked Jenna up and spun her around. He placed a relatively chaste kiss on her lips, clearly mindful of the children watching them. Regardless, it still started a fire deep in her core, and she couldn't wait until they were alone. Cade would stoke the flames within her as he always did. She didn't doubt that fifty years from now, it would still be the same. Thank goodness, he was a fireman.

PART SIX

STUD MUFFIN

"This shit's got to stop," Rafe Montoya muttered to himself as he stared across the hotel lobby. "That can't be her."

For the past eight months, any petite woman between the ages of twenty-five and forty-five, with long, black hair, and curves in all the right places, reminded him of Dr. Suki Ralston. He'd only known the FBI criminal psychologist for a few days, after she'd been called in to help on a serial killer case in Dare County, North Carolina, where Rafe was a state police investigator. He and his partner, Brian Malone, had been assigned to assist the local sheriff and an FBI agent who just happened to be Brian's brother, Sean, who'd requested the psychologist develop a profile on the killer. Suki had walked into the conference room and sat right down on Rafe's heart without even knowing it—it'd been lust at first sight for him. Now, every time he caught a glimpse of a woman who looked similar to her, thoughts of having her naked in his bed popped back into his head. It was crazy. He'd never even kissed her—hell, he'd never even taken her on a date or anything. All he'd done was silently drool over her, while waiting for an appropriate moment to ask her out—being in the middle of the gruesome case hadn't made things easy. Unfortunately, she'd returned to Quantico before an opportunity arose and to get to know her better.

Yeah, he probably could've asked Sean for her phone number —the FBI agent was good friends with her—but the bastard had been busting Rafe's chops over the woman ever since he'd caught him eyeing her ass. Rafe could've also tried to contact her at the FBI headquarters in Quantico, but the distance between where they both lived and the fact that neither of their careers were conducive to long-distance relationships had held him back. He had a feeling that if he ever got Suki into his bed, he'd never want to let her go. The problem was he couldn't get her out of his mind and couldn't stop seeing her wherever he went.

He was in Aspen Springs, Oklahoma, for the weekend to attend his cousin's wedding. While Rafe had never met Jared's fiancée before, he was looking forward to reconnecting with some of his extended family and a few friends he hadn't seen in a while. They'd all made the trip to the bride's hometown for the nuptials.

As he was about to tear his eyes away from the Suki look-alike's shapely ass, the woman turned around and Rafe's cock twitched. Holy hell, he hadn't been mistaking her for the real thing this time. There she stood, the woman who'd starred in more fantasies than Rafe wanted to admit to having lately. Of all freaking places he could've run into her, Aspen Springs hadn't been anywhere near the top one thousand. His mouth watered. Damn, she was as gorgeous as he'd remembered. Her Korean/Hawaiian heritage gave her flawless, caramel-colored skin, beautiful brown eyes, and dark, silky locks he wanted to plunge his hands into. She stood five-foot-three in her bare feet, but Rafe had only ever seen her in high heels, which made her legs look a mile long. Her curves were meant to be explored by a lover's hands and mouth, and Rafe was jealous of any man who'd ever had the pleasure of seeing her naked.

His gaze slowly climbed upward from the tips of her white, open-toe wedges, over her sexy-as-sin legs, before lingering a little longer on her hips, and then her breasts, which were covered by a simple, teal dress. Hanging from her shoulder was a black & white, canvas, tote bag. When he reached her face, butterflies in his stomach took flight when he found her smirking at him, her eyes dancing with mirth. As she sashayed toward him, cheesy porn music played his head.

"Well, well, well, fancy meeting you here, of all places. How are you, Rafe?"

Having her recognize him and remember his name did something for his ego, and his cock twitched in his jeans again. He smiled. "I'm good, Suki. How are you doing? You're not here for work, are you?" He doubted it, considering when he'd met her, the attire she'd worn had been very professional. Now, she looked nothing like an FBI agent with a doctorate.

"I'm doing very well, and no, I'm not working. I'm actually here for my college roommate's wedding."

No way! He couldn't get this lucky, could he? "You mean Stacey?"

Her trim eyebrows shot up. "Yes! How did you know?"

"Jared's my cousin."

A laugh escaped her luscious mouth, and he felt it all the way to his toes. "Oh my God! What are the odds?" She gestured to his suitcase on the floor next to him. "I take it you haven't checked in yet, hmm?"

It took a moment for him to stop staring at her plump lips, the ones he wanted to kiss more than taking his next breath, and comprehend her last question. "Um . . . yeah . . . no, no, I haven't. I'm in line." He glanced over his shoulder to see said line for the front desk had disappeared and he was standing in the middle of the lobby like an idiot. His cheeks heated as his gaze returned to her amused one. "A line which is no longer there."

"Hey, Suki! Hate to make you leave the stud muffin standing there, but the shuttle's here!"

Chuckling, she rolled her eyes, then twisted to eye the group of women she'd been with. "Way to be subtle, Jules."

"When have you *ever* known me to be subtle, Suk?" her friend retorted, using an abbreviated version of her already short name.

Suki shook her head and turned back to Rafe with a huge grin on her face. "Sorry about that. We've all matured quite a bit since college but put us together in the same room and we regress a bit."

"No worries." Being called stud muffin was both a tad condescending and a boost to his ego so they canceled each other out.

"We're headed to the hot springs for a few hours. Care to meet up in the bar later? That seems to be where everyone will be around four o'clock for cocktails before dinner."

A brief flare of arousal at thinking she wanted to have drinks alone with him was dashed when she mentioned "everyone" would be there. Still, he wasn't passing up an opportunity to get to know her outside of a work setting. "Um, sure. Four o'clock sounds great."

"Great," she repeated, removing a pair of sunglasses that'd been resting atop her head. "I'll see you then."

As she left to join her friends, Rafe tried to keep his gaze off her ass since her friends were watching him with interest. Giving them a quick wave, he grabbed his suitcase and stepped toward the reception desk to check in. The weekend looked like it was going to be more fun than he'd expected. A lot more fun.

ALL AROUND HER, her sorority sisters chatted as the shuttle drove them to the hot springs just outside of town, but Suki couldn't concentrate on any one conversation. Her heart was still pounding in her chest. Of all the people she'd expected to run into in Aspen Springs, Rafe was at the bottom of the list. Not that she minded. Nope! Not. At. All.

Holy hell, he was as gorgeous as she'd remembered—possibly even more so. When she'd first met him, it was during a meeting of the task force that'd been put together to catch the Seaside Strangler. He hadn't been the only handsome member of law enforcement in the room that day, but he'd been the one she'd developed a growing attraction to. What she wouldn't have given to have been able to stay a few extra days in Whisper, North Carolina, all those months ago, just to find out if the hunky investigator was as interested in her as she'd been with him. But duty had called, and she'd been needed back in Quantico. The only other time she'd been back to the small town on the Outer Banks since then was to visit with Sean and his fiancée, Grace, and Rafe had been away. Sean had told her Rafe's mother had suffered a minor heart attack while vacationing in Florida with friends, and he'd flown down there to be with her at the hospital before driving her back home in her own car.

Suki had felt a kick to the gut when she'd heard the news. She'd wanted to call Rafe back then and ask how his mother was doing and let him know she was praying everything would turn out all right. But she'd chickened out. They'd only known each other for a little over two days, months earlier, in the middle of a serial killer investigation. What would he have thought about her calling him out of the blue? Would he have even remembered who she was? Well, now she had her answer. She'd been shocked when, after Jules had told her some hottie had been eyeing her legs and ass, to turn around and see the man who'd starred in many of her fantasies of late. When she'd seen the flash of recognition in his eyes, along with a heavy dose of lust that couldn't have been misinterpreted at all, she'd felt a swirling sensation in her core. It'd taken everything in her to stride confidently across the room without a "holy hell, come fuck me, baby" look on her face or drool seeping out of her mouth.

He'd been wearing a navy-blue golf shirt, a pair of jeans, faded in all the right places and hugging his trim hips and muscular thighs, and white sneakers. He hadn't shaven yet today and the course stubble on his jaw had made her palm itch to touch it and let it rasp against her skin. He stood a yummy six feet one inch—Suki loved tall men—and his dark brown hair that was almost black, and wicked hazel eyes completed the very handsome package.

"So, Suk! How do know Mr. Stud Muffin back there?" Jules Bennett shouted from several seats back on the shuttle bus. "Please, tell me you tapped that fine specimen!"

She rolled her eyes, surprised her friend had waited this long to ask about Rafe. "He's a state police investigator I met on a case in North Carolina. We had a strictly professional relationship."

Across the aisle, another sorority sister, Morgan Ackerman chimed in, "He sure as hell wasn't checking you out like a professional—unless he moonlights as a male escort."

The rest of the group roared with laughter and put their two cents in about how hot they thought Rafe was and that if Suki didn't want him, they would be more than willing to take him on.

"All right, all right. Settle down, my bitches." Might as well head everyone off at the pass, so they didn't start playing matchmaker between her and Rafe. This was one time she didn't want or need her wingwomen to interfere. "Yes, I think he's hot. Yes, I've had a few fantasies—well, more than a few. And yes, I wouldn't mind turning them into reality. So chill. I'll definitely be doing some flirting and getting to know him better this weekend. And if I get a chance to tap that, well . . ."

Her friends hooted and hollered at her unfinished sentence. This was how it always was when "the girls" got together, but, many times in the past, Suki, and probably a few others, had stretched the truth a little bit when it came to men she'd dated. Suki had been in several relationships over the years, but one-night-stands weren't her thing. The very few she'd had in college had left her feeling empty, even though she'd known going into them things would be over come sunrise. But there was something about Rafe that drew her in. She wanted the man, there was no denying that. If all he was willing to offer her was a night or two, could she accept that and go with it? Before the question fully formed in her mind, she knew the answer was yes. Never had she fantasized about a man as much as she had these past few months since meeting Rafe.

Thankfully, the van they were in pulled up to the entrance to the hot springs, and everyone's attention was diverted—well, everyone except Suki's. She still had Rafe on her mind and didn't think that would change any time soon.

GRABBING HER BEIGE, clutch purse, Suki took one last look in the full-length mirror in her hotel room. For once she was grateful for her habit of packing a few extra, just-in-case outfits. She'd been on enough trips, for business and pleasure, over the years to know plans could change at the drop of a hat, and, therefore, she needed her available attire to be flexible. "Be prepared" wasn't just a Boy Scout motto, it was Suki's maxim.

Instead of the light-weight, gray, A-line skirt, with a white, sleeveless top, she'd been planning to wear tonight, she put on a red, Michael Kors dress that stopped just above her knee. The halter top bared her shoulders and molded her tits, but not too snugly. Simple earrings, a bracelet, and her grandmother's wedding ring on her right hand were all the jewelry she wore. On her feet, a pair of nude high heels completed the sexy yet classic look. Since she would be having her hair in an updo for tomorrow's wedding, she'd left her long locks down. The strands were as smooth as silk, and she wondered if Rafe would want to run his fingers through them. Maybe he'd wrap them around his wrist and pull her head back before lowering his own to kiss her. Their lips would touch, and she'd open her mouth, inviting his tongue to plunge inside for a taste. *Damn, it's hot in here!*

After making sure she had her room key, phone, and lipstick, plus some cash and a few other necessary items, Suki opened the door and strode out into the hall. Immediately, wolf whistles filled the air. The bride's brother, JT Gramme, and two of his cousins were walking toward her, presumably on their way to the elevators. JT's voice rang out. "Damn, woman! I swear you get sexier looking every time I see you. Are you sure I can't convince you to marry me?"

Suki chuckled. If she didn't know him as well as she did, she might have blushed at his words. However, JT was gay and not the least bit interested in marrying her, or even sleeping with her, which would never happen even if he did swing in her direction. She loved Stacey's younger brother like he was her own, having gotten to know him well when he'd attended the same college they had, yet a year behind them.

She waited until the trio reached her, then fell in step next to JT, putting her arm around his waist as he placed his over her shoulders. "You know it would never work out, babe. We're far too much alike."

"Damn straight," he replied with a single nod of his head. "We're both sexy as sin and love to shop, check out men in tight Wranglers, and watch Magic Mike while eating Häagen-Dazs and French kissing the pillows."

Letting her go, he did a little dance, pumping his hips ala Channing Tatum, which caused one of his cousins to groan. "TMI, cuz!" Suki wasn't sure which one had spoken since the identical twins were behind her. She'd only met Jeremy and

Adam a few times over the years through Stacey and had to be looking directly at the two men to be able to tell them apart.

Chatting, they rode the elevator down together, then strode into the hotel's bar where they separated. Music from a jukebox and multiple conversations filled the air. Suki's gaze sought out Rafe and immediately zeroed in on him standing with several people at a nearby pub table. As if he felt her eyes on him, he turned and spotted her. His eyes widened in admiration and lust before a sexy grin spread across his face. His gaze dropped to her toes then slowly wandered up her body until it reached her face once more, and Suki felt a warm, tingling sensation all over.

While he'd been taking her in, she'd been doing the same. He was wearing a pair of brown loafers, dark-blue jeans, and an ivory, button-down shirt with the sleeves rolled up to his elbows, showing off his muscular forearms—swoon! Some women got turned on by a guy's smile, eyes, broad shoulders, etc., but, for Suki, sinewy arm porn did something to her every freaking time.

When she realized those arms were coming toward her, along with the rest of the incredibly sexy man, Suki lifted her gaze to his again. His eyes smoldered, and the one dimple he had, on the left side of his mouth, had her wanting to lick it.

"You look beautiful," he said, stopping in front of her. He took her hand and brought it to his lips, kissing her knuckles. That simple, chivalrous gesture heated her blood and dampened her thong panties.

"Thank you. You're looking very handsome yourself."

They stood there staring at each other for a few moments. While, to some, it might have seemed awkward, but to Suki, it felt like foreplay. And, damn, did she love foreplay—especially the non-physical kind that came with mentally sparring with an intelligent man.

Rafe was the first to break their eye contact, but his gaze didn't go far, dropping a few scant inches to her lips. In an unconscious act, she licked them and was amused and turned on further when Rafe let out a low growl. "Damn, woman, you're killing me here. Before I say to hell with it, sweep you up in my arms, and take you up to my room to ravish you, can I buy you a drink?"

Well, it was nice to know she wasn't the only one on the edge of making a rash decision, like inviting him up to her room before they had a chance to get to know each other better. Rafe was apparently all too aware of their physical attraction, just as she was. What was it about this man that had her wanting to throw caution to the wind? She had the urge to screw first and ask questions later, something she hadn't done with a man since college. But, back then, she'd been sowing her wild oats, out from under the watchful eyes of her parents and older brothers for the first time in her life.

"Sure."

When he gestured toward two empty stools at the bar, she sashayed over and took one, completely aware of the fact Rafe's gaze had been on her ass until she sat. While one-night stands weren't her thing, she had the flirting and seduction routines down pat for times just like this. She wasn't a tease, but when she found a man she was interested in, she knew how to garner his interest.

Instead of sitting, Rafe stood beside her, facing her, and leaned against the bar. He flagged down the bartender, then raised an eyebrow at Suki in an unspoken question. She responded, "A Pinot Grigio, please."

Rafe turned back to the waiting man dressed in a white shirt and a black tie and pants. "A Pinot Grigio for the lady, and I'll take a Guinness, please." As the bartender left to get their drinks, Rafe returned his attention to Suki. He slowly shook his head as his eyes roamed her face. "Damn, woman. Have I told you how beautiful you look?"

She smiled broadly. "Yes, you have, but I'm not averse to you repeating it."

"Well, then . . ." He cupped her jaw with one hand and caressed her cheek with his thumb. "Let me do just that. You are a very beautiful woman—one I'd like to get to know a lot better. I've thought about you often since we met. You're impossible to forget. Please tell me I'm not the only one who wants to know why the air crackles with electricity every time we're in the same room."

The desire in his eyes flustered her—something that rarely happened. Her parents raised a strong, confident daughter, but Rafe Montoya made her week in the knees. Thank God she was sitting down.

Before she had a chance to agree with him about the electricity, tomorrow's bride and groom joined them. Jared slapped Rafe on his back. "Hey, cuz."

With obvious reluctance, Rafe dropped his hand. "As usual, Jar, you have lousy timing."

His cousin's eyes narrowed in confusion. "You two know each other? How?"

Stacey lightly smacked Jared's arm. "I told you a little while ago—they met on that serial murder case he was involved in a few months back. I swear you only hear half the things I say to you."

Her fiancé leered at her. "And what was I doing when you told me that?"

She put her arms around his waist and gave him a swift kiss. "It was when you were undressing me with your eyes after I came out of the shower wearing that blue, silk robe you love."

"Enough said. Stop looking so fucking sexy, and I'll start paying attention to what you say."

Suki rolled her eyes at Rafe. "They're disgusting, don't you think?"

He chuckled. "Quite. But for that response, Jared gets to keep his man-card."

"Of course I do—I know how to hold onto that baby," his

cousin responded. He placed a kiss on his fiancée's lips. "And I know how to hold onto this baby too." His gaze flittered to something over her shoulder, and he muttered a curse. "Oh, shit, Stace, your Aunt Margaret is coming this way. Save me."

"Eep!" Without any hesitation or a goodbye, Stacey grabbed his hand and pulled him in the other direction.

Rafe frowned after them then looked at Suki. "Did I miss something?"

Giggling, she waited for a round woman in her mid-sixties, dressed to the nines with a heavily made-up face, to walk by and out of earshot. "Stacey's aunt seems to have a bit of a crush on Jared. She always greets him with a big, wet kiss on his cheek, leaving a lipstick smudge, and a hug that's a *little* too long for his comfort." She held up her thumb and forefinger about a quarter inch away from each other. "She's a cougar on the prowl, but don't worry . . ." Clutching the collar of Rafe's shirt, and with a twinkle in her eyes, she pulled him closer. "I'll protect you."

A grin spread across his face as he settled in next to her, putting a hand on her waist and the other on the bar. "As a state police investigator, I'd normally be offended by that promise, but, in this case, I'd be a fool not to accept it."

"Good." Slipping her fingertips under the edge of his shirt in the space separating two buttons, she ran the fabric between them and her thumb. A sexy lilt was added to her already husky voice. "Now, I believed you wanted to know something before we were interrupted."

HOLY HELL. Thank God his hips were between the bar and Suki's crossed legs, because Rafe was able to hide his erection from her and the rest of the room that was filling up with wedding guests and others staying in the hotel. He'd gotten hard the moment he'd spotted her—hell, he'd been semi-hard waiting for her—but now he was in pain, wanting her more than any woman he'd ever met. There was no denying the fact she was doing some serious flirting with him, and he thanked his lucky stars. He would have been devastated if she wasn't interested in him.

Rafe wasn't egotistical, but he'd had more than his fair share of women over the years. He'd never had a hard time charming them and getting them to agree to a few rolls in the sack. He'd had a few one-night stands, but usually when he found a woman he was attracted to, he wanted more than just one night—but he'd never found a woman that had made him want beyond that. There had been a few women he'd dated for several months, trying to see if there was the connection needed for something long term, as in marriage, but none of the relationships had panned out. His cousins and friends all seemed to have found the love of their lives, and Rafe wanted that too. Honestly, he'd hoped he would have been married with several kids by this point in his life. He was halfway through his thirties and still single. But as he waited for Suki to continue her side of the conversation, he found himself hoping he'd finally found "the one."

At some point, the bartender had set their drinks down in front of them, and Rafe picked up his beer and drank just enough to wet his suddenly parched throat. Suki's fingers continued to fiddle with his shirt as she took a sip of her wine. Setting the glass back on the bar, she continued. "The air does seem to crackle when we're together. Why do you suppose that is?"

He stared at the mouth he wanted to kiss more than anything. "I don't know, but I'm all for trying to find out."

A new song began to play on the jukebox, and Rafe immediately recognized the song by Foreigner. Hearing "I Want to Know What Love Is" seemed kind of ironic. He had a feeling he could very easily fall head over heels for Suki—hell, he was probably halfway there.

Putting her hand on his forearm, she slid off the stool. "Dance with me?"

Never in his life had he been so grateful that his mother had taught him several styles of dance growing up. She did it for a living, but, thankfully, she'd given him lessons in the privacy of their home. He would've been teased mercilessly by his friends otherwise.

"It would be my honor." He signaled the bartender. "Place our drinks behind the bar, please. We'll be back in a little bit." It might seem like a paranoid request to some, but Rafe had seen far too many people regret their assumption that nobody would spike their unattended drinks.

After the bartender acknowledged him, Rafe took Suki's small hand in his and led her to the bar's small dance floor where several other couples had decided to put it to use as well. Pulling her into his arms, he didn't bother leaving any space between them, flattening his hands on her lower back. Without hesitation, her arms went around his neck as he moved them around in time to the music. He couldn't keep his gaze off her face, reveling in the desire he saw in her eyes, knowing she could see the same in his.

Her fingers played with the short hairs at his nape, sending goosebumps skittering across his skin. "You're a very good dancer. I'm impressed."

He smiled. "Thank my mom. She made sure I'd never step on a woman's toes on the dance floor."

"I wish my prom date had gotten lessons from someone. He came close to breaking several of my toes that night."

Rafe spun them in a tight circle to prove his next words. "No broken toes for you tonight. I can even dip you if you like."

Her brow shot up. "Wow. It's been a long time since I've been dipped. In fact, the last guy that tried it nearly dropped me on my ass."

In one smooth motion, he slid one hand to her upper back, pivoted, and dipped her with an expert flare. The heat in her eyes increased tenfold when he said, "Trust me, sweetheart, there are plenty of other things I'd rather do to your ass than drop you on it."

Lifting her back up, he returned both hands to her lower back and pressed her into his body, letting her feel how much he wanted her. Normally, he wouldn't have moved that quickly with a woman he barely knew, but Suki was different. The time she'd spent in his head all these months made her seem closer to him. The way she didn't object and appeared to cuddle even closer to him told him she felt the same. As much as he wanted to whisk her upstairs and rock her world, he forced himself to slow down, at least, a little bit. The night was still young—hell, they hadn't even had dinner yet—but he was determined to make sure Suki ended up in his bed before the weekend was over.

SUKI SMILED when Rafe put his hand on her lower back in a possessive yet sensual manner as he spoke to his aunt and uncle. After their heavenly dance earlier, she and Rafe had returned to the bar and retrieved their drinks. More wedding guests joined the growing crowd in the bar, and the two of them spent the next two hours conversing with many others, but they stayed together, side by side. Suki didn't mind that they weren't alone because she found herself learning more about Rafe in a relaxed setting, without having to play twenty questions. She was able to fill in a lot of blanks about him just by listening to him talk to others. He was an only child, and his own parents hadn't been able to make the trip from North Carolina because his father was recovering from hip replacement surgery, following a fall. Rafe was very close to his dozen or so cousins, and they all took pride and pleasure in busting each other's chops and trying to best one another. She was surprised to learn he had a law degree he planned to fall back on once he retired from the state police. Although he loved his job in law enforcement, and wasn't leaving it anytime soon, he occasionally did some pro bono work on the side through a friend's private practice. As long as there weren't any conflicts of interest, his supervisors had given him the okay to moonlight.

Rafe was a die-hard Baltimore Orioles' fan and swore he was going to take her to one of their games sometime, after she told him she'd never been in any of the major league ballparks in her life. He'd cringed when she told him she was technically a Yankee's fan—mainly because her father and brothers were. Honestly, she couldn't name a single player on that year's team— it'd been so long since she'd sat with her family and watched one of the games. Rafe was now determined to convert her into a Bird's fan.

The more time she spent in his presence, the more her attraction to him grew. Not only was he sexy as hell, he was kind, funny, intelligent, protective, and respectful. All combined, he was a man she could easily fall in love with. But she was nervous about that. Yes, they both had the hots for each other, that was beyond obvious, but what if all Rafe wanted was a weekend fling? It was almost a four-hour drive between her apartment near Quantico and where he lived in Greenville, North Carolina—not exactly convenient for a relationship, if he even wanted one with her.

Argh. This was the part about dating she hated. Trying to figure out what exactly the guy wanted out of a relationship. Despite having her doctorate in criminal psychology, Suki tried hard not to overanalyze a guy's interest in her. If a few dates turned into something more, then she'd think about where they were headed and if he could be "the one." Several of her friends had said they knew the moment they met their significant others that they were "the one." Others said it had taken some time for them to figure it out. Then there were a few whose "forever" radars had given false readings and they were now facing divorce.

Suki felt someone sidle in next to her and glanced over and saw it was Jules. The two women were going to be bridesmaids tomorrow, along with their other friend, Morgan, Stacey's two younger sisters, and her childhood friend who'd been named the maid of honor. Jules gave Suki a little hip check. "A bunch of us are going to some pub up the street called The Dog & Duck for dinner. Why don't you and the stud muffin join us?"

Beside her, Rafe snorted. His aunt and uncle had moved on, and he'd apparently overheard Jules's question. "What's with the nickname, ladies? I'm starting to feel like a breakfast treat."

"That's because you *are* a breakfast treat, darlin'," Jules teased with a flirtatious laugh. "In fact, you're yummy enough to be a lunch treat, dinner treat, and midnight snack too. Please tell me you have a brother who looks just like you."

When Rafe blushed at the unveiled compliment, Suki giggled and rolled her eyes. "Enough, Jules. And, no, he doesn't have a brother." She eyed Rafe. "If I promise my friends will be on their best behavior and knock off the 'stud muffin' remarks, would you like to join them for dinner? I don't know about you, but I'm getting kind of hungry." Before her friend could give a snarky response to that, Suki gave her a "please shut up" glare, which Jules reluctantly obeyed.

Just as Rafe opened his mouth to reply, three of his cousins walked up, and one slapped him on the back. "Rafe, man, we're heading down the street to The Dog & Duck. You in?"

Rafe chuckled as his gaze shifted from his cousins to Suki and Jules. "Let's go. Ladies, after you."

Rafe, Suki, and about two dozen other wedding guests spent the next four hours in the crowded pub, toasting the soon-to-be newlyweds with shots, beer, wine, and karaoke. The latter had been either pretty darn good or really off-key, depending on who was singing. Falling into the off-key group—she would only sing with a bunch of friends—Suki had been pleasantly surprised when Rafe had gotten up on the small stage and sung lead on "The Boys Are Back In Town," with three of his cousins backing him up. The crowd had gone wild, clapping and cheering. A few female wolf whistles had rung out too. Suki hadn't known Rafe could sing that well and wondered what other surprises were in store for her as she continued to get to know him better. If she hadn't already been lusting after the man, the sexy wink he'd given her at the end of the song would have pushed her over the edge in a heartbeat.

Suki was very aware most of the women in the bar were eyeing the Montoya cousins, like they wanted to jump their bones, but his eyes had been on her for almost the entire night. The only time he'd looked away for more than a moment was when he'd been talking to his cousins and a few of the other people in their large group. But when that happened, he'd either held her hand, spread his hand across her lower back, or put his arm around her waist and pulled her into his side. Anyone who didn't know them would think they were an item—a fact Suki had no problem letting them believe.

As they stood there talking to Jules, Morgan, and JT, Stacy and Jared joined them. The groom slapped his brother-in-law-to-be on the back. "Stace and I are heading back to the hotel. We'll see you all in the morning."

When the couple left, Suki glanced around and noticed a few others from their group were getting ready to head out. She suddenly realized how tired she was. It'd been a long day. She'd arrived at the hotel around 11 p.m. last night after her flight had been delayed out of D.C. Then she'd ended up on a secure video conference call with FBI agents in Seattle who'd needed her opinion on a homicide. They'd been trying to identify a serial rapist/killer who'd been leaving bodies within a hundred-mile radius of the city over the past two years. Yesterday, a female victim had been found murdered, with some similarities to the UNSUB's MO, but there'd been a few differences that had seemed out of place from his prior kills. After getting the details of the homicide, Suki had concluded that this wasn't one of the UNSUB's victims, and the agents should look closer at the victim's family, friends, and acquaintances for her rapist/killer. Whoever he was, he'd tried to make it look like she'd fallen prey to the Emerald City Slayer—God, Suki hated when the press came up with nicknames for serial killers.

As a result of the half-hour video conference call and the notes she'd needed to type into her computer before crawling into bed, Suki had slept only a few hours before waking up when her internal clock had loudly announced it was 7 a.m.

She tried to stifle a yawn, but Rafe caught her in the act and smiled. "I better take you back to the hotel. You've had a long day and have an even longer one tomorrow."

That was a bit of an understatement. He'd been listening earlier when the maid of honor had rattled off the pre-wedding agenda for the next morning, which included sitting for one of the hairstylists and a makeup artist who'd been hired to make sure the bridesmaids looked their best. Then, once everyone was dressed, there would be an insane number of pictures they had to pose for—and those didn't include the ones which would be taken with the full bridal party *after* the ceremony. This was the seventh wedding she'd been a bridesmaid in over the years, and if she ever got married, Suki wanted to elope. There was just too much stress in doing it any other way.

"As much as I hate to admit it, you're right—I'm beat. But you don't have to walk me back. Stay and hang out."

He shook his head. "Nope. I'm actually bushed myself."

Suki doubted that—he'd looked like he was having a great time and could stay longer—but didn't argue since she really did want him to escort her back to the hotel. She wasn't ready to say goodnight to him just yet.

After saying their goodnights to those who were staying behind, Rafe took Suki's hand and led her through the crowded bar toward the exit. There, he released her, held open the door for her, and then joined her on the sidewalk, grasping her hand again and threading their fingers together. Warm, fuzzy feelings travelled up Suki's arm and spread throughout her body. Damn, her attraction to the man had increased ten-fold throughout the evening.

"So, Doc, any interesting cases lately?"

She smiled for several reasons—his calling her "Doc," he was the only one currently in Aspen Springs that she could discuss her work with, and it was the first time all day he'd asked her about it, aside from when they met in the lobby earlier. "Several, actually. I was up late last night with the Seattle office." As they strolled toward the hotel, she told him about the serial killer and two of the other cases she was consulting on, leaving out anything that was confidential. Several times, when she mentioned the victims, Rafe squeezed her hand. It was as if he knew that she wasn't as unaffected as she tried to seem. Suki had learned long ago to maintain a professional image with her expressions and body language when discussing some of the worst and vilest human beings that had ever walked the planet, slaughtering people with no remorse.

After they rode the elevator up to her floor and reached her room, Suki pulled out her key card and hesitated. She looked at Rafe, who was standing beside her with his hands in his pockets. She couldn't tell what he was thinking, although she had a pretty good idea. It was probably what she was thinking—inviting him in would lead to him not leaving until the morning. She was torn. There was no denying her attraction to this man, but Suki needed to pull back and regroup. She had to be certain this thing between them was more than a weekend fling. If it was, then she'd rather it didn't happen. She was falling for Rafe and didn't think her heart could stand it if he didn't feel the same.

She went with a half-truth. "If I didn't have to get up so early in the morning and run around like a chicken without a head, I'd invite you in."

In silence, Rafe stared at her face intently for several moments. She wasn't sure what he was searching for and was about to ask what was wrong when he took a step closer, then cupped her chin with one hand. His eyes gleamed with a combination of desire and understanding. "I had a feeling this was where tonight was going to end, and I'm okay with it. Disappointed but okay with it. However, I'd regret it even more if I didn't do this."

His gaze never left hers as he slowly lowered his mouth toward hers. He paused as if making sure she wanted the kiss as much as he did. *Hell, yeah!* Going up on her tiptoes, Suki brushed her lips across his. That was all the encouragement Rafe needed as he pulled her closer and devoured her mouth. Neither cared that they were standing in the middle of the hallway where anyone could walk by and see them or where they could be caught on a security camera.

Suki let Rafe turn and pin her against the door to her room. She loved the taste of him as he slid his tongue into her mouth to wrestle with hers—whiskey, spice, and all man.

Her hands went behind his head to his nape where the tips of his hair tickled her fingers and palms. Clutching her hip with one hand, his other plunged into her hair, angling her head where he wanted it. His mouth left hers, kissing along her jawline to the sensitive tissue behind her ear. Suki was all too aware of his erection bulging against her lower abdomen and mons. She gasped for air, knowing she had to stop the delicious yet insane makeout session but, at the same time, not wanting it to end.

Down the hall, the elevator doors opened, and several people exited the car, laughing and chatting. Rafe stiffened and lifted his head to glance at the group. Suki followed his gaze, grateful to see the hotel guests' retreating backs as they headed in the opposite direction.

Suki and Rafe were both breathing heavily, and he rested his forehead against hers. "I was hoping for a brief goodnight kiss, but that was far better."

She smiled. "I agree."

Taking a step back in obvious reluctance, Rafe grasped her hand and lifted it to his mouth, skimming his lips across her knuckles. "I'll see you at the wedding. Save a dance for me?"

Feeling saucy, she responded, "Oh, I think I'll pencil you in for quite a few of them, if that's okay with you."

"To hell with a pencil—ink them in."

THE RECEPTION WAS in full swing, everyone celebrating the nuptials and toasting and roasting the newlyweds. A DJ was cranking out tunes that had most of the guests hitting the dance floor. Rafe was having a great time, but his mind conjured up deliciously dirty thoughts every time his gaze found Suki.

Until the wedding ceremony and photo sessions were over, he hadn't had more than a brief chance to touch her or talk to her all day—touching her was what he'd wanted to do the most. After she'd entered her hotel room, alone, last night, he'd made sure he heard her engage the door's deadbolt before taking the stairs up to the next floor where his own room was located. Stripping out of his clothes, he'd jumped into the shower and taken care of his raging hard-on. While he'd hoped she would've invited him to spend the night in her bed, he was glad she hadn't. Suki was different than any other woman he'd ever dated. The more he got to know her, the more he didn't want to do anything to screw up their budding relationship.

Now, he couldn't keep his eyes off her. All the bridesmaids wore the same navy-blue color, but their dresses were designed differently, in a style that suited each best. Suki's was a one-shoulder, floor-length sheath that made him want to go nibble on her exposed shoulder. It accentuated every curve, and more than once, Rafe had fought the urge to go deck some guy who was drooling over her.

In between her bridesmaid's duties during the reception, she joined him often. They'd shared several dances and partied with everyone else. He'd noticed she alternated drinking wine spritzers with glasses of water, and he'd followed suit with his beer. If the way she'd been flirting with him tonight was any indication, he wouldn't be just escorting her to her hotel room door—he'd be spending the night behind it, in her bed. He wanted to make sure alcohol wouldn't put a damper on his performance later, because that would really suck.

Both were leaving tomorrow afternoon for the airport and their respective flights home. Rafe was determined to have set plans to see her again before they parted. One night with Suki was not going to be enough for him, of that he was certain. Hell, a hundred nights wouldn't be enough.

Just as one of Rafe's cousins approached him with a new bottle of beer for both of them, the DJ cut the music and announced it was time for the bride to throw the bouquet. All the single women were to join her on the dance floor to find out if they were the next to get married, as the tradition went. Suki and several of her old college sorority sisters were among the women who loosely lined up opposite the bride who turned her back toward them. As the photographer and videographer got set to capture the moment, the rest of the guests loudly counted to three.

The floral bouquet went up in the air, over the bride's head, toward the waiting group of women. Hands went up amid squeals and laughter. The bouquet bounced around then one hand grabbed it and held it up in the air in victory. Rafe chuckled when he saw Suki's triumphant grin as she showed off her prize.

A chair was brought to the center of the dance floor, and Stacey sat while her husband teasingly removed her garter from under her dress before kissing it, then spinning it around with his finger. The DJ called for all the single men to gather for a chance to catch the garter. *Oh, hell no!* Rafe would be damned if any other man got that scrap of lace to put on Suki's bare leg. Leaving his full beer on a nearby table, Rafe joined the group of men, ranging from ages seventeen to over sixty, on the dance floor. He jockeyed for a good position as Jared faced the DJ and prepared to throw the blue and white garter over his head.

At the count of three, the garter flew into the air. All around Rafe, men dove for it, although a few only made a halfhearted effort. After being jostled, Rafe thought he'd missed his chance, but the piece of lace fell from another man's hand when someone's arm hit it. The garter landed at Rafe's feet, and he snatched it up before anyone else could grab it. He held it in the air, then his gaze found Suki's, and he winked at her. A sexy, saucy grin was her response.

The chair was once again brought to the center of the floor, and, this time, Suki sat in it. The music came back on and "Danger Zone" from *Top Gun* filled the air. *Oh, yeah, baby.*

Rafe removed his suit jacket and tie, then rolled up the sleeves of his shirt to his elbows, all the while laughing, eyeing Suki, and getting the crowd riled up. A beautiful blush stole across Suki's face, but she was clearly enjoying his striptease and antics as she yelled, "That's right, stud muffin! Take it off!"

Her sorority sisters hooted with laughter and, more or less, repeated her words. *Stud muffin.* Okay, there could be far worse things they could be calling him. He could deal with it, especially since, in a few moments, his hands were going to be under the skirt of Suki's dress. *Hell, yeah!*

Dropping to his knees a few feet away from her, he crawled forward, his gaze on her amused one. Laughter and wolf whistles rang out in the large room once more, loud enough to be heard over the music. When he reached her, she uncrossed her legs and set one foot on his thigh, careful not to dig the pointed heel into his flesh. He cupped her ankle and lifted it so he could put the garter around her foot.

The guests shouted in unison, "Higher! Higher!" Rafe was more than happy to oblige their demands.

Sliding the piece of satin and lace up over her ankle, he placed her foot back on his thigh. Grasping part of her skirt, Suki pulled it upward, exposing more of her calf. Rafe glanced up and winked at her. "Thank you, darlin'. But that's high enough. I don't want anyone else to see what my fingers are itching to touch."

Her eyes widened in surprise at his teasing and boldness, but then she leaned forward and tapped her index finger against the underside of his chin. She lowered her voice so only he could hear her. "Bring it on, stud muffin."

Damn, he liked the nickname much better when she said it in that sexy, husky voice. "With pleasure."

He dragged the garter up her calf and under the hem of her dress. He loved how soft and silky her skin felt against his fingertips. His dick twitched in his pants, and he cursed himself for taking off his suit jacket.

"Higher! Higher!"

God, if he went much higher, he'd have a full-blown hard-on —as it was, he was already at half-mast. Thank God his suit pants had some room in the crotch.

Lifting the garter above her knee, he caressed the skin of her inner thigh and was thrilled to see her eyes fill with lust. Good thing he wasn't the only one affected by the public scene, but to do what he wanted to do to Suki, Rafe wanted to be somewhere without an audience.

Despite the crowd's demand, Rafe halted the garter's advance. After giving Suki's thigh a squeeze, he pulled his hands back out from under her dress and gave her another wink. Standing, he held out his hand and when she took it, he helped her to her feet.

He leaned forward and put his mouth near her ear. "Don't think this is over, Doc. I look forward to pushing that garter up as far as it will go."

Surprising him, she went up on her tip-toes and pecked his cheek before saying, "I'm looking forward to it too."

Fuck, yeah!

SUKI'S HEART pounded in her chest as she and Rafe rode the elevator up with several other people. She'd wanted to get him alone all day but more so since his funny, sensual tease with the garter. If his fingers had gone any higher under her skirt, he would have found her thong damp. Her clit had pulsated to the point she thought she'd have her first public orgasm—not something she wanted in the middle of a wedding reception with all eyes on her.

When they reached her floor, he squeezed her hand then led her out to the hallway after the doors slid open. Suki knew he wouldn't be leaving her at her door again tonight, and she knew *he* knew it too. Checkout was at noon tomorrow, so that left them eleven hours to enjoy the hell out of each other.

As they approached her room, Suki let go of Rafe's hand and retrieved the key card from her clutch purse, then handed it to him. He unlocked the door and gestured for her to go in first. The door clicked shut as she tossed her bag onto the dresser and kicked off her shoes. Her toes curled into the rug in relief at being released from their confines. The shoes had been comfortable, but she'd been in them for over thirteen hours.

Before she had a chance to turn and face him, Rafe's arms went around her waist, pulling her against his torso and rock-hard erection. His lips caressed the side of her neck, then kissed their way down her exposed shoulder. Shivers went down Suki's spine as she ground her ass against his cock.

"Mmm," Rafe murmured. His mouth moved to her ear. "Before I start undressing you and consuming your delectable body, tell me this is what you want, baby. I don't want any misunderstandings between us. If I have my way, this won't be a one-night stand. When we get back home to our respective realities, I'm going to figure out ways to see you again. I'm not going to be satisfied with just one night."

Suki fell for him a little more in that moment. Slowly spinning around, she lifted her gaze to him. It felt odd seeing him so much taller than she was since she was no longer wearing her heels. Desire burned in his eyes, as hot as it burned in her own. She ran her hands up his chest and clasped them around the back of his neck. "I'm glad to hear that because I don't think one night is going to satisfy me either. I want you, Rafe, here, now, all night. No misunderstandings. Just two consenting adults who are wildly attracted to each other."

He growled seconds before he crushed his mouth to hers. Parting her lips, Suki welcomed his tongue into her mouth where it explored every inch it could reach. His fingers found the zipper of her dress between her shoulder blades and lowered it until it stopped just above the small of her back. He dragged his fingertips up both sides of her spine until they got to the top of her dress. Parting the material further, he peeled the garment from her torso. It skimmed her body and dropped to the floor, leaving her standing there in a lacy, strapless bra and a matching thong, the same color as the dress, and the white and blue garter. She stepped out of the garment, toeing it to the side.

Taking a step back, Rafe eyed her from head to toe and back again. He surprised her by dropping to his knees, clutching her hips, and pulling her toward him. Leaning forward, he lashed her nipple with his tongue through the lace of the bra. Heat pooled in her core as she felt her panties become wet with her desire. His hands moved to her ass, squeezing the globes and holding her in place.

Suki reached back and unhooked her bra, tossing it to join her dress on the floor. Rafe growled again before sucking her nipple into his mouth. Molten lava coursed through her as she grabbed his hair, running her fingers through the dark, silky strands and holding his head to her breast.

As he continued to suckle her nipple, teasing the taut peak, his hands dropped to her hips and found the straps of her thong. He pulled the skimpy piece of lingerie and the garter down her legs, then helped her step out of them. Rafe's mouth switched to her other tit, and one of his hands went between her legs. He moaned into her flesh when he found her wet and wanting. Suki's clit throbbed with need.

He glanced up. "Take down the bun, baby. I love it when your hair is down."

Reaching up, she quickly removed the clip and pins holding up the thick strands until they fell over her shoulders and down her back. The corners of Rafe's mouth ticked upward. "Fucking gorgeous."

Pushing her back a step to give himself some room, Rafe lowered his head, kissing her abdomen until he reached her bare mons. His tongue flicked her clit, causing Suki to gasp and beg for more. He obliged until she swayed on her feet.

Rafe growled, stood, and then swooped her up into his arms before laying her out on the bed like a feast. "Damn, you are so beautiful," he said while almost ripping the buttons off his dress shirt. "More beautiful than you were in my fantasies. Although, you were pretty damn hot in them too."

Yanking his shirt off, he tossed the garment to the floor, then kicked off his shoes while unbuckling his belt. Within moments, he was gloriously naked. His thick cock stood long and proud against his abdomen. Rafe was well-endowed, and Suki had a moment of concern wondering if she'd be able to take him. But all thoughts flew from her mind as the man crawled over her, licking and nipping his way up her torso to her neck.

Wrapping her arms around him, Suki pulled him down so she could feel his weight on top of her. When her breasts made contact with his skin and chest hair, her nipples tightened to the edge of pain. Suki moaned in delight when Rafe found one of her erogenous zones on the side of her neck with his mouth. She scratched his back, and he groaned. "Fuck, yeah. Love that."

They became a writhing mass, and she couldn't tell where Rafe ended and she began. He slid to her side and dragged his hand down her body to her pussy which was dripping with need. When he ran his fingers through her soaked folds, she bucked her hips, silently demanding he put his fingers inside her. Rafe obliged with one and then two fingers, thrusting them deeper with each pass. His mouth closed around her closest nipple, and he bit down lightly then lifted his head, taking the peak with him. At the same time, he ground the heel of his hand against her sensitive clit. The combined assault sent Suki's orgasm rushing to the surface. "Oh, God! Yes! Oh, Rafe!"

As she tumbled into a seemingly bottomless pit of ecstasy, Rafe didn't let up. Before she realized what was happening, another orgasm hit her. She rode wave after wave until she collapsed on a beach of bliss, gasping for air. *Holy shit! Back to back orgasms!* That had never happened to her before—not one on top of the other. Rafe turned her on and made her body sing in a way no other man had ever done.

After his mouth and hand slowed then stopped, Rafe raised his head, and a sexy smile spread across his face. Suki pushed on his shoulder until he rolled onto his back. "My turn."

His grin broadened, but he didn't say a word. Leaning down, Suki kissed his muscular chest, giving each taut, brown nipple some attention with her tongue. Rafe's hand plowed into her hair, tugging the strands and lighting up her scalp. The pain was exquisite, fueling her desire.

Suki nipped and ran her tongue over his hard flesh, following the trail of coarse, dark hair down his abdomen. When she reached his impressive erection, she lifted her gaze to his. She oh-so-slowly swiped her tongue across the tip, savoring the salty pearl of pre-cum she found there. Rafe's hips came off the bed. "Oh, fuck! Lick me again, baby. Please don't stop!"

Sucking the dark purple tip of his cock into her mouth, she pleasured him. The hand in her hair pushed and pulled, setting the pace Rafe wanted. He moaned, gasped, and begged, and knowing she'd done that to him gave Suki a heady feeling.

"Shit!" Rafe grabbed her under her arms and pulled her up his body, forcing her to release him. When she straddled his hips, he held her pussy against his throbbing shaft. "Sorry, Doc, but if I'd let you continue, things were going to be over far too soon. I want to be deep inside you when I come."

She smiled and scored her nails down his chest, enjoying how his nostrils flared as he growled. Reaching down, Rafe grasped the base of his cock and ran the tip against her labia. Rising higher on her knees, she asked, "Condom?"

His eyes grew wide. "Holy shit! You've got me so crazy, I forgot—and I never forget. Sorry. There's some in my wallet."

Suki scrambled off him and the bed, located his pants, and retrieved the black, leather wallet as Rafe said, "Behind my shield."

She took that as consent to open his wallet and get them. Pulling out three square, silver packages, she chuckled. "Either you're very optimistic or you were a Boy Scout."

Shrugging, he grinned. "Both."

Placing the wallet and two condoms on the night stand, she kept the third one and used her teeth to open it. She crawled back onto the bed and straddled Rafe's thighs. Taking the small, latex disc, she set it on the head of his cock and rolled it down the length of his solid flesh. She then shifted forward until her knees were on either side of his hips. Holding Rafe's cock upright, she sank down onto him, swaddling him in her wet heat. Suki rocked back and forth, rising and lowering herself again as she slowly took every inch of him until she was seated as far as she could go.

Rafe's eyelids were at half-mast and his jaw was clenched. Grabbing Suki's hips, he lifted her before slamming her back down onto his shaft, over and over again. Resting her hands on his chest, Suki rode him hard, using her thigh muscles to help him maintain a fast pace.

Her third orgasm was slower than the first two, but just as potent. The walls of her channel rippled around his cock, drawing a curse from his mouth. "Fuck! Ah, baby, what you do to me."

Her gaze never left Rafe's, relishing the intense passion she saw in his eyes. He'd told her the truth earlier—this wasn't a one-night stand they were having. It was so much more.

Suki's head swam in a post-orgasmic euphoria. Rafe rolled them until he was once again above her. Grasping her leg by the back of her knee, he lifted it toward her chest, opening her further. He pounded into her for a minute or two, then plunged in and held himself, stiffening as he emptied his seed into the condom. Moments later, he collapsed on top of her.

Rafe put his mouth to Suki's ear. "I hope I didn't tire you out, sweetheart, because we're going to be doing that many more times tonight—at least two more times. Hell, I might have to run out for some more condoms."

SUNLIGHT PEEKED around the edges of the closed curtains, waking Rafe. He glanced at the beside clock and snorted when he saw the time. He couldn't remember the last time he'd slept so late, unless it had been after an overnight shift. Cuddled next to him, Suki stirred. "What time is it?"

"Twenty after nine," he replied.

"Wow, I never sleep this late."

"Join the club."

They both stretched out the kinks that had settled into their muscles after their marathon lovemaking. While Rafe hadn't run out for more, they had used the last of the condoms from his wallet.

Pulling her into his arms, Rafe said, "What do you say we take a shower, then go have some breakfast before heading to the airport? We still have plenty of time."

Suki snuggled into his side. "Mmm. In a few minutes. I don't want to get up just yet."

Silence filled the room for a few moments as Rafe hesitated before speaking again, unsure of what her response would be in the morning light. "When can I see you again?"

Her head shifted until she made eye contact with him. "That's not just something you're asking because it's expected, is it?"

"What? That I want to see you again? Hell, no, baby—it's not something I just blurt out because of morning-after awkwardness. I really want to see you again, but I know with the four-hour drive and our schedules, we're going to have to plan to see each other in advance and deal with it if one of us has to cancel at the last minute." He cupped her chin and caressed her cheek with his thumb. "I can't help but feel there's something between us—something special. Something real. I want to see where it goes and hope you feel the same way."

She smiled, then turned her head to kiss his palm. "I was kind of hoping you'd say that. You're right—it might be hard—but sometimes I could come to you, or you could come to me. Maybe sometimes we could meet halfway. To answer your question, yes, I want to see you again."

"Awesome." After kissing the top of her head, he threw the covers off them, stood, and then tugged on her hand. "C'mon, Doc. Let's take that shower and start making plans."

Chuckling, Suki climbed out of bed and followed him while admiring his taut ass cheeks. "Anything you say, stud muffin."

Suki and Rafe first appeared in *Her Sleuth: Malone Brothers Book 2*, and I knew I'd be revisiting them one day. Get to know KC, Sean, and Brian Malone, and their family and friends. You never know who will fall in love next when the new Whisper Softly series rolls around!

Also by

Samantha Cole

***Denotes titles/series that are only available on select digital sites.
Paperbacks and audiobooks are available on most book sites.

THE TRIDENT SECURITY SERIES

Leather & Lace

His Angel

Waiting For Him

Not Negotiable: A Novella

Topping The Alpha

Watching From the Shadows

Whiskey Tribute: A Novella

Tickle His Fancy

No Way in Hell: A Steel Corp/Trident Security Crossover (co-authored with J.B. Havens)

Absolving His Sins

Option Number Three: A Novella

Salvaging His Soul

Trident Security Field Manual

Torn In Half: A Novella

***Heels, Rhymes, & Nursery Crimes Series
(with 13 other authors)

Jack Be Nimble: A Trident Security-Related Short Story

***The Deimos Series

Handling Haven: Special Forces: Operation Alpha
Cheating the Devil: Special Forces: Operation Alpha

The Trident Security Omega Team Series

Mountain of Evil
A Dead Man's Pulse
Forty Days & One Knight

The Doms of The Covenant Series

Double Down & Dirty
Entertaining Distraction
Knot a Chance

The Blackhawk Security Series

Tuff Enough
Blood Bound

Master Key Series

Master Key Resort
Master Cordell

Hazard Falls Series

Don't Fight It
Don't Shoot the Messenger

The Malone Brothers Series

Her Secret

Her Sleuth

Largo Ridge Series
Cold Feet

***Antelope Rock Series
(co-authored with J.B. Havens)
Wannabe in Wyoming
Wistful in Wyoming

Award-Winning Standalone Books
The Road to Solace
Scattered Moments in Time: A Collection of Short Stories & More

***The Bid on Love Series
(with 7 other authors!)
Going, Going, Gone: Book 2

***The Collective: Season Two
(with 7 other authors!)
Angst: Book 7

***Special Collections
Trident Security Series: Volume I
Trident Security Series: Volume II
Trident Security Series: Volume III
Trident Security Series: Volume IV
Trident Security Series: Volume V
Trident Security Series: Volume VI

About

USA Today Bestselling Author and Award-Winning Author Samantha Cole is a retired policewoman and former paramedic. Using her life experiences and training, she strives to find the perfect mix of suspense and romance for her readers to enjoy.

Awards:

> *Wannabe in Wyoming* (co-authored by J.B. Havens) won the bronze medal in the 2021 Readers' Favorite Awards in the General Romance category.
>
> *Scattered Moments in Time*, won the gold medal in the 2020 Readers' Favorite Awards in the Fiction Anthology category.
>
> *The Road to Solace* (formerly *The Friar*), won the silver medal in the 2017 Readers' Favorite Awards in the Contemporary Romance category.

Samantha has over thirty-five books published throughout several different series as well as a few standalone novels. A full list can be found on her website.

Sexy Six-Pack's Sirens Group on Facebook
Website: www.samanthacoleauthor.com
Newsletter: www.geni.us/SCNews

facebook.com/SamanthaColeAuthor

instagram.com/samanthacoleauthor

bookbub.com/profile/samantha-a-cole

goodreads.com/SamanthaCole

amazon.com/Samantha-A-Cole/e/B00X53K3X8

Made in the USA
Columbia, SC
30 May 2024

35977904R00102